I0664033

# PRAIRIE

# PRAIRIE

Nicollette Petrou

Copyright © 2022 by NICOLLETTE PETROU

All rights reserved. No part of this book may be reproduced in any manner whatsoever without written permission except in the case of brief quotations embodied in critical articles and reviews.

Dedicated to my mother, Joanne,
who believes in happy endings.

# Chapter One

————————————

## Digging for Answers in Mud

Henry Gilchrist caressed the horse's mane, to distract it from the ridiculing voices that screamed in a foreign tongue from the cellar, but there was only one person down there. The coarse hair slipped through his scarred hands. They were branded from countless days of work. His fingers throbbed with ache but it was a somewhat pleasant escape from the screams nearby. The yell subsided to a whisper. It was now drowned out by the rain which dropped from the roof and clanged along the pipes. The innocent words were suddenly interrupted by a voice that roared with agony before it diminished into silence.

He peered over his shoulder at the town of York. Between the trees and green terrain, he made out the hipped roofs and smoke trails. The stone walls of the Minster cathedral reached towards the twilight sky. The countless windows watched him from afar and listened to the ungodly screams. At over three-hundred years old, the Minster would have witnessed many sinners before but had they all been forgiven?

The argument made no sense but Henry listened anyway. He stroked the gloss mane of the horse, named Ginny. Her hooves stomped in the mud which dampened Henry's tailcoat and silk stockings. His blistered hands tightened at the bridle around Ginny's muzzle. Her grey eyes were filled with anguish as she searched the paddock before she focused on the words whispered into her ear. The voices stopped and the cellar was silent. For now, they found peace.

Henry waited for Ginny to cease whinnying and preoccupied himself with a stick, which he used to pick at the ground. Mud melted away to reveal a green weed. He encircled the greenery with his stick and pushed the soil aside. The plant inhaled the air but the leaves were glued to the ground with each pelt of rain. Henry stood beside the shrub as he was forced to listen to the wailing voices.

He peered up, the black curls clung to his neck, inevitably sticky from the rain. A sweat-laden droplet trickled along his nose and slipped into his mouth. The taste was as salty as the argument that echoed through his ears. Henry's head pounded. He had forgotten how many days it had been since the yelling had started. There seemed no point in counting anymore. It was endless. He left the paddock and strode towards the Georgian house. Rain clattered against the wood and the paint peeled off the walls. The clay tiled roof was lined with gray gabled windows. A speckled English Setter trailed at his heels. It's nose scoured his pants and it whined. The Setter circled him, it jumped through the mud and barked.

"Hush. Stay here."

Henry's woollen coat reeked of wet dog. It weighed down his arms as he opened the front door. The rain pelted nearby but he was sheltered by the doorway, where speckles of light glowed from the arched fan window. He entered, then removed his boots. Henry's feet itched from the wet socks and the fibres of the knitted carpet didn't help. He strode past the drawing room, where the bitter stench of animal lard emitted from the tallow candle.

Mother brewed a pot of green tea and presented a mug to each of the three ladies who were engaged in conversation. Their flamboyant laughs echoed through the room and mother bore a grin. Her cone shaped skirt danced across her heels and there was a hole in the silk that was freshly sown. She bowed, to which Henry tilted his hat. Mother only invited her friends over at dark. Emery's screaming generally subsided by nightfall. He suspected this was the case because the cellar was dark at night and so she was lulled to sleep. Or maybe she slept from fear of the dark.

Henry disappeared inside the dim house. Inside the kitchen he pulled open the oak handle of the icebox. The smell of dried fish thickened the air and a glob of butter clung to the door handle. The ice block had melted almost halfway and he now stood in a puddle of water that was laced with the scent of stale food. He grabbed the butter and slammed the door, rattling the frame. Henry turned around to see Father now stood before the arched sink.

"Replenish the ice," he muttered.

Father rinsed a linen towel under the sink and nurtured an unusually swollen hand. Excess water dripped along his sleeve but he was too preoccupied by the pain to realise. "I won't repeat myself."

Henry raked his fingers through his black hair and began to turn away when he noticed a fresh hole in the green panelled wall, where a cockroach crawled inside. "That wasn't there this morning," Henry said.

He examined the hole. Only something heavy could cause that much damage. Then Henry realised, Father punched the hole in the wall. It did not happen often, but when Father's temper got the best of him, you were glad to have not been in the way.

Beneath the punctured wall he grabbed a slice of bread from the bread bin. He gnawed on the edge but was hardly able to tear off a piece. Henry dipped the bread inside the oily butter and began to devour dinner. It tasted like lard on a dry biscuit; rather than bread and butter. The stale bread was lodged between his teeth when a shriek cut through the air. Henry distracted himself by the view outside the window. Paint peeled away from the wooden frame and moss tracked the outskirts. The scream distorted the serene farmland, the horse's ears twisted and their hooves trampled the ground. They searched for the threatening source but were confronted with empty space. They galloped through the paddock, on a quest for safety. Naive creatures, there was no danger.

"What is your plan, Father? You cannot keep her locked down there forever."

"I know. She will be taken away for medical treatment."

Henry's blood curdled within his veins. Hope for Emery dwindled but so long as she breathed, she would continue to fight the illness. He pulled away from the window. Offloading their burden would not ease the stigma. It would follow the family wherever they walked and so, the town would never forget the Gilchrist family. They were cursed. Doomed. Even the cathedral shunned them. The priest was at a loss for answers. He instructed the family to get rid of Emery and the evil spirits, it was the only way to set them free of their burden. It made sense. After all, there was no reason for the rest of them to be dragged away from their faith. He couldn't blame Father for wanting to detach himself from the spell. Henry even agreed to some degree. But there was a speckle of pity. A faint glimmer of hope that normality could return. He despised himself for thinking outside the guidance of the cathedral. In a sense, he sided with Emery's demonic possession. But there had to be a way through the darkness.

"Disease has eaten her mind. She has been cast down by a spell, a demon's doing. There is nothing we can do." Father wrapped the linen cloth around his hand and tied a knot, as he walked towards Henry. Gin lifted from his coat and Henry followed the alcoholic fumes. He was not wrong. Demonic possession was permanent. "I will grant you and your brother peace from the beast."

"Don't call her that." Henry swirled the bread in the oil butter film. Even a demon's work could be undone. There had to be a way, she just needed more time.

"You defend her. Why?"

"Because she is my sister and your daughter."

"Not anymore."

"I think we should try another purge. It almost worked last time."

Father's hazel eyes didn't waver. He stared at Henry, a son that was nothing like him. Henry knew nobody had overcome insanity but there was a way, it just had to be found. Emery was encased inside her mind that was decaying but she was alive.

Father sighed and rubbed the space between his eyes. "You consider yourself a holy man but you are selective with what you hear. The priest recommended Emery be sent to the asylum. To rid our family of this curse and you pretend that never happened. I taught you better, did I not?" Father asked.

Henry listened to the truth.

"Don't judge me for this. You're making things harder," Father said.

"Do not take the absence of my words as judgement. Now, excuse me, Emery will be waiting for dinner."

The dome entrance of the cellar was filled with darkness and a pitiful lamp that illuminated the far corner. The air tasted of mould and a whimper echoed off the brick walls. Henry extended the candle in search of the source. He followed the light trail that glowed before him. "Emery, it's me."

"Urian?"

"No, it's Henry."

"You sound just like him."

"We are twins." He crouched down and Emery scuffled across the pine floor. Strands of ragged hair draped around her face. She reached toward the stale bread when Henry noticed small cuts along her hands.

"What is this?"

"I don't remember," Emery mumbled through a mouthful of food. She pressed her scrawny shoulder against Henry and was relieved to have company. "How was the prairie today?"

Henry glared at her confused. "The what?"

"Prairie. Did you see anything interesting?"

"There is no prairie, we live on a farm. What are you talking about?" Henry grew impatient.

Emery rolled her eyes and chuckled. "You make me laugh. Just like all the other North American citizens."

"We are almost four thousand miles from North America. We are the same distance from a prairie. You are sorely mistaken."

The nonsense conversation brewed a rage within Henry's stomach. It was fools' talk. But he was no better. Conversing about the non-existent prairie only fed the hallucination. The cathedral would be disappointed in him to say the least. Henry changed the topic. "You were screaming before."

"Yes. There was a lady here and she was whispering ungodly things in my ear."

Henry lifted Emery's chin. Her broken brown eyes were dull and crumbs lined her cheeks.

"It was only you down here."

"No it wasn't." Emery gnawed along the edge of bread as though she had eaten rocks. She used both hands to hold the meal and her fingernails were filed back, to reveal stubby nail beds.

"Emery, you are seeing things that are not real. You are manifesting lies."

"I am not lying, I'm telling you the truth."

"Stop it. You are sick, your mind is ill. Nobody was down here. You were alone and you put on an act. You spoke in two tongues. Now, I need you to listen to me before Father sends you away."

Emery stopped eating. Her breathing slowed and she lifted her gaze. Her pointed nose sniffed the air. "Do you smell that? It's horrible down here."

"You won't have to smell it for much longer. Finish your dinner. I will be back tomorrow."

"Do not leave me!" Emery clutched Henry's arm and her knuckles bulged. Her teeth chattered and bread dropped from between her lips. She peered around the cellar. "It's dark at night."

At fifteen, Emery was too young to be sick. There was no cure and her future was pitiful. He gulped down his sorrows towards her. Henry pulled away, there was nothing more to be said. He walked across the cellar and stood in the doorway when he heard whispers. "What are you doing?"

"Talking to the voices. It's a good one this time."

Emery giggled, her mind became more twisted by the day. Henry swallowed against the lump in his throat and shut the door.

A burst of embers broke from the fireplace and the room was uncomfortably warm. Henry lowered his head to inhale the aroma of the cellar; sweat and soil drifted from his shirt. Despite the stench, Emery's presence remained and it filled him with hope. Although it was too much to comprehend.

He pulled the shirt off and his pale, freckled chest was shielded by a dressing screen. He slipped into a sleeved red-and-white striped top instead. The crackle from the fireplace laughed at him and was a reminder of Emery, the voices she whispered to and the meaningless conversations. Maybe it was all a fib and there were no voices. *Did she make it all up? If so, I would be just as mad as her, for believing such lies.*

He attended the buttons on his shirt and recalled the memory from earlier that day, of the heartbroken screams and the contorted voices. There was nothing he could do. Maybe his Father was right.

Henry walked towards his bed, where the velvet curtains hung from a brass rail. He drew the covers to his shoulders. His eyes shut but his mind raged with questions. There was no plausible explanation to Emery's delusions and he wondered how she had been cast down by such a spell. Henry felt along his stubbled jaw in thought. He tossed about the idea of how Emery spoke in another language. He couldn't make sense of where she would have learned it. English was her native language but she spoke with confidence in a foreign one. It baffled him that Emery was petrified of the voices by day yet laughed with them at night. It was madness and if Henry dwelled on the thought for a moment longer, he would also be condemned to insanity. The fire cackled, as if it too, spoke in another tongue.

# Chapter Two

----------------·

## Winter Whispers

An August breeze rustled the crisp leaves and they danced across the farm. Sunrise glowed over the house and blinded Henry, who stood in the doorway and greeted the ice delivery men. They steered the horse-drawn carriage that was loaded with ice blocks of about 30 pounds each. Bold letters across the side read 'pond ice,' fresh from the warehouse. The wooden wheels pulled to a halt and the driver twirled his mustache. He tilted his hat. "Good morning sire," he called.

"Thank you again for the ice," Henry replied. He accepted the delivery and loaded the ice box with a fresh block before he ventured into the farmland. He wore a sack coat with a tattered shirt and silk boots.

Henry tightened the bridle around Ginny's muzzle. Her black mane was braided into Elk knots along her back. He tightened the straps when Urian appeared with the other horse, who bore a distinctive white streak across its face. Urian extended his hand and the handshake was shared. As Henry's twin brother, Urian looked completely different; from the pin-straight hair to the chestnut eyes and scrawny physique. The only resemblance was, well, their sideburns.

The twins attached the bridle to the hook of the plough and started their day at dawn. The horses strode across the farmland and upturned the soil. Henry's hands tensed around the plough handles as he followed their guide. The rope that tied the plough to the bridle straightened as it pulled forward and the rusted iron creaked. Henry's hair was slicked into a ponytail, secured by a black bow. His neck broke into a sweat.

Urian reached inside his pocket and watched Henry from the corner of his eye. "Would you like a cigar?"

"If you ever had a cigar, I doubt you would allow me the pleasure of smoking it."

"You don't believe me?" Urian asked, baffled.

"When was the last time you could afford a cigar?"

"Last week." Urian lifted his hands to his mouth. He held nothing but air between his fingers and pretended to puff away. His lungs filled with clean air and he blew out. He glanced over and the twins chuckled. The most tobacco smoking they ever did was inhale the pleasurable fumes of passersby. It was a cheap alternative.

"Listen, Urian, one day, when our crops earn triple our current wage, I will purchase a tobacco factory. I'll even let you sniff the fumes from outside."

The twins laughed until their breath gave out.

The jokes never grew old. The twins fantasized about the expensive pleasures of life since they were eight-years old, when they started to help on the farm. They would plough beside Father, with their floss hair and wide smiles, chatting about things they could not afford; butlers with tailored coats, ruby rings, polished shoes and farming coats that actually fit.

"Have you heard?" Urian asked as he ploughed, seemingly with ease.

Henry's emerald eyes glared at him. The topic sounded important but the news had slipped by him. Urian clenched his jaw. Something wasn't right.

"About Emery."

Henry loosened his grip and almost tripped over the plough. He instinctively bent his elbows to stop from falling over.

"Emery is going to leave soon. Mother told me this morning."

"When?"

"In a few days. She needs help, surely you can see that."

"Urian. We can't let them take her."

"I'll admit, the thought of losing her is horrid but I don't see another option. She has condemned herself for talking to evil whispers. She should have known better. If only she listened to father, none of this would have happened."

She couldn't be sent away in a few days. It was too soon. Emery needed more time. She needed treatment. Henry pulled against the tunic that tightened around his throat. Perhaps he misjudged Emery but he couldn't fathom her unfortunate future. She deserved more, at fifteen and still a child. "Urian, we must help her."

"How can we do that?"

"The masquerade is tomorrow night."

"Do not get any ideas."

"Mother and Father will be distracted." Henry grabbed Urian's shoulders and pulled him in. "I am going to help her."

Urian jerked away and re-arranged his hands on the plough. "How do you suppose you will do that? You are not a doctor!"

"Will you help me?"

The familiar scream blared through the farmland. Henry turned towards the Georgian house, where the air stood still. The panelled windows were dim, Emery was left to rot in the cellar, a prisoner to the confines of her own mind. She screeched again and this time the dog ran from behind the house. It barked at the front door and reared onto its haunches. The horses pushed forward and the plough forced Henry to focus on the task at hand. A fragment of his heart chipped away. He didn't have the stone-cold heart of a young man and like Emery, he too, would be an outcast.

"You're weak, Henry. Nothing can be done to save Emery. She will go where the rest of them do, to-"

"Don't say the name," Henry cut him off.

The York Retreat. A pleasant name to cover up the fact that it was really a lunatic asylum. Henry never witnessed the asylum but heard tales of it; the brick walls and cream trimmings that contained secrets that were better off forgotten. Nobody ever came out of York Retreat, or at least, nobody that Henry knew. That was not a cure. It would be another confinement, just like the cellar where Emery was now.

Urian jabbed Henry in the chest. "I heard old man Winchester got sent to that asylum just the other day. As his son dropped him off, he had the opportunity to peek inside the front door."

Henry's curiosity got the best of him, as he stared at his twin. He begged to know more.

Urian continued. "The screams were of a hundred people, Winchester's son said. They begged for mercy as the nurses bound them to chairs. Their hands were shackled and the hallway was dim, filled with endless shadows. The saddest part of all, a small hand made it's way through the blackness. Two beady eyes looked out. He was just a boy, around five years old." Urian shrugged. "I heard someone yanked the child back inside, right before they took Mister Winchester. I don't think we will ever see him again."

The tale rattled Henry's spine. Each story was more horrific than the next. "So there it is. The awful tales of the asylum and you would let our sister go there?" Henry asked.

"There is nothing left of Emery, she is only a shell. A host, a carcass. She looks as you remember but -" Urian tapped his temple. "There is nobody home. She's not coming back, Henry."

"For a twin, you think nothing like I do."

"That goes both ways," Urian puffed.

The twins walked across the freshly ploughed soil. Henry's cotton gloves reached inside a bag and grabbed a handful of garlic seeds. A winter breeze blew and Henry waited for it to pass before dropping the seeds into the ground. Urian nudged his elbow.

"I think our work is almost done for the day. Now, please elaborate on this plan of yours."

Henry turned towards him. The sarcasm grew old, as did his patience.

"You never let me answer your question. I didn't accept or deny your plea for help. I will help you."

"You will?"

"Of course! She is only a girl, not to mention our sister."

Henry stared at his brother. As if through a mutual understanding, he felt the desire within. He studied his face and his eyes beamed with sincerity. Urian was being truthful.

Henry sowed another handful of seeds into the ground, from which, the fresh mulch seeped into his nose. "At the masquerade tomorrow night, when the moon is up and the night is dark, I will take Emery away. I will ride with her into the land and we will find shelter. I think somewhere peaceful would serve her justice. Somewhere new and unfamiliar, where I can try herbal therapy and maybe another purge. The doctor recommended a change of air which could help, the wilderness has clean air. We never tried the bleeding out technique or leeches. There is so much that hasn't been explored. I will return once she is healed and make our parents proud once again."

"Do you think this could work?"

Henry tossed the final handful of seeds into the ground. His arms shook with uncertainty. There was no guarantee Emery could be redeemed but he had to try. It was the least he could do. He glanced up at the sky and sighed, dusk was upon them.

"I will return for dinner but there is something I must do first," Henry said. He tilted his hat to Urian and turned to leave.

Henry walked along the outskirts of the wet road and circled the potholes. His silk shoes were tarnished with dried mud and his toes were chilled by the road. Damn it. There was a hole in the bottom of his shoe. It would make the journey longer.

Evening fog cleared to reveal the town of York. A young boy carried the handle of a rusted lantern along the road. His blonde hair poked from beneath the cream hat which matched his cloth coat. His black suspenders reached his shoulders. The boy lit the roads for travellers. Henry knew better than to venture into town at night but he assured himself it would be a short trip.

The bustle of York was virtually silent and eerily dim. The roads were almost bare, for not many people dared to travel at dusk. Horse-led carriages navigated through the town and the clatter of hooves tramped the uneven roads. Henry noticed a few children lit up the road and from a distance, the lanterns were like fireflies.

The entrance to the Minster of York loomed ahead and Henry stopped walking. He tilted his hat to the two-hundred-foot-high cathedral. The limestone-rock structure was positioned among a bed of leafless trees. The dormer windows poked out from the tower and Henry wondered if someone watched him. He looked upright at the rose glass above the entrance. Although the night concealed the Minster's beauty, he still remembered the thousands of stained glass fragments; blue, ruby, emerald and yellow, that would reflect the moonlight. The glass petals shadowed him as he ventured inside.

Henry sat into one of the empty pews but despite the Minsters' colossal size, he was one of the few people inside. He faced the altar, where the tall windows were known as the five sisters were. Their slender glass bodies reached towards the wooden roof. The main room filled with tall walkways and the smallest movement echoed throughout the cathedral. Henry looked at the octagonal roof which appeared in the formation of a star and joined the beams along the walls. Gold rails trimmed the glass fragments of the star which covered the roof. The cathedral was dim and Henry sighed, he suddenly regretted the decision he would soon make.

"Forgive me, father, for what I am about to do. I am not turning my back to you but simply desperate for help." Henry clasped his hands together and felt the scars and blisters along his fingers. His palms pulsed with pain but it was pitiful compared to the sinful act he had in mind. "What I am about to do tomorrow night is for the love of my sister." His nose tingled and tears crept into his eyes. He knew Emery had turned away from her faith and spoke to the disease within her mind. It was her own fault and even a purge wasn't enough to bring her back. The last thing Henry wanted was to be condemned for saving her. He ignored the advice by the priest; to sentence his sister to an asylum for she welcomed evil into the home. He was doing the opposite of what he should be. Henry choked on a lump at the back of his throat. He was torn in half; save Emery and face the sinful consequences or let her go and remain a faithful man. He was forced to make a decision but so was Urian. If his twin had chosen to save Emery, that offered some comfort. Henry's choice was justified but still, he pondered what would come of him. After he saved Emery, what would the cathedral think?

"Please, forgive me."

Henry peered around the Minster, in the row behind him was a man dressed in black. He stared ahead with blue eyes that didn't blink. It was the town baker who, despite his daily produce of fresh bread, was masked by something else. His cracked lips drew apart and he whispered to the stained glass. Henry couldn't help but wonder what the baker's sins were. Henry rubbed his eyes, his mind was made up. He decided if he confessed his plan to the Minster, it would lessen the sin.

"Tomorrow night, I will take Emery away from the house. I will ride with her into the land and although I do not know when we will return, I hope to bring her back as she once was."

Henry waited in the Minster, although he wasn't sure what for. Perhaps a sign or answers but nothing ever came. He walked towards the front doors and as he left, realised the baker had already disappeared. Nightfall encompassed York and the children that lit the streets were sparse. Henry followed the light of one of the firefly lanterns and made his way back home.

# Chapter Three

----------------

## Behind this Ceramic Mask

Henry sat beside the lantern on the cellar floor, when Emery crept out of the shadows. She cradled the tea and pressed the silver rim against her lips, allowing the steam to blow over her face. Her bottom lip dripped with blood and it dyed the drink red.

"What have you done to yourself?"

Emery sipped the tea and winced as it scorched her throat. "Have you not noticed it has been quieter around here? The screaming is only at night. If I bite my lip, I cannot scream and maybe then, Father and Mother will think I am cured and … Set me free."

"You punish yourself." Henry buttoned the sleeve of his sack coat. He produced a handkerchief and dabbed at Emery's lip, it was swollen and purple. "You're not doing yourself any good."

"I will be punished either way for my sick mind, what's the difference if I bring it upon myself?"

"You won't be taken away. I have a plan."

Emery's eyes fixated into the darkness over Henry's shoulder. Her hands shook and waves of hot tea to spurt over the edges of the cup. She sunk her rotten teeth into her bottom lip and frowned at the pain. Her whine grew louder and cheeks puffed up.

"Look at me," Henry clasped his hands around her cheeks. Emery's freckled skin was clammy. Her jaw shifted as she bit harder into her lip.

"Look into my eyes," Henry urged.

Emery did as she was told and her eyes appeared to bulge out of her sockets. A tear trickled down her cheek and Henry leaned forward. "Don't look away, look at me. Just breathe."

Emery spat out saliva from between her pressed lips. She stared at Henry and her face crumpled with discomfort. She dug her teeth further into her lip.

"Focus on me, look into my eyes," Henry reassured. He slid his hands over her ears and pressed down softly. He blocked out the voices from the cellar and Emery's panting soon dropped to normal breaths. It was a placebo, for the voices were inside Emery's head but it worked. Her lips drew apart and air flowed into her mouth. Henry watched his sister come back to reality.

"I have a plan to take you away from here," Henry

whispered. "The masquerade is tonight and York will be distracted. When the moon is up, Urian and I will come back for you. The three of us will ride into the night and I promise to keep you safe."

"There is no cure, the voices told me so," Emery whispered.

"The voices are not real. I will make you see that. Don't ask me how but I will find a way."

Emery flung her arms around Henry's throat. She dug her weeping fingernails into his coat. Her tears evaporated into Henry's tunic and clung, like raindrops, to his sideburns. He planted his nose into her shoulder, to the Heavens, he hoped his plan would work. "I have to go now."

"But how will I know when you're coming back?"

Henry pointed to the lantern. "By the time the candle runs out, I shall be back, with Urian and the horse."

After a day of ploughing and sowing broccoli, Henry lured Ginny into the stable yard by a narrow corridor. The gag-worthy aroma of manure and body odour drained the air from the stable. He rubbed the horse's muzzle and stripped away the dirt from the day. Henry dunked a cloth in the bucket of water and scrubbed the animal. Excess droplets slid into its eyes and the gelding stepped backwards. Henry's blisters pressed against the cloth and his hands began to ache. His mind drifted away from the pain, he had to act normal but the more he tried, the harder it seemed. If his parents caught onto the plan that night, all hope would be lost. He would never be able to try again and Emery would be gone for good. Henry played out the plan in his mind; first he would attend the masquerade and when the floor was occupied by the York town that danced the night away and the moon was high above, he would slip aside. Only then would it be safe to take Emery.

Henry finished cleaning the horse and started to polish the bridle. He dunked the cloth into the pale of water and scrubbed away the dirt from the straps. Urian appeared and reached for the other bridle. "Today is the day. Are you ready?"

"Of course." Henry's stone cold face gave nothing away. He held his head high and masked the chills that rattled his spine. He had no idea how they would fix Emery but he refused to speak of the uncertainty.

"Tomorrow would be Emery's last day in York. Tonight would be her last night until she would be taken away to the asylum. It would be her new home but not anymore because we can change that." Urian winked as he scrubbed the bridle. "What will you do if this doesn't work?"

The comment caught Henry off guard. He twisted the cloth around his fingers. "I don't know." He rubbed away the water and stared at his calloused hands. Dirt was wedged beneath his nail beds and no matter how hard he cleaned them, the filth was stuck. "How could it not work? Tonight is the best night to escape. Have Mother and Father caught on?"

Urian stepped back. "No, of course not. I'm just saying time is running out. Tonight is the only chance we have."

Henry sighed. He switched his gaze to the sky outside the window. Twilight was among them and the plan would soon be in motion. "We better get back to the house. The masquerade will start soon."

Wild primrose flowers and shrubs bowed before the pleasure gardens, more-so they were squashed by the crowd. Gas lamplights marked the perimeter and glowed over a crowd of children who played with the water fountain as people hustled around the gardens. The women of the masquerade held onto their husband's elbow, as did mother. Her harlequin mask was white and detailed with bright blue, green and gold. Her pinchbeck necklace and rings glistened under the moonlight, although constructed of nothing other than inexpensive copper and zinc, she flaunted the cheap jewellery. It matched the grace of her dress. She almost hopped into the masquerade, with excitement. Father looked particularly smart in his pierrot white and black mask. It created an exquisite contrast from his orange coat and emerald leggings. They disappeared within the garden that was crowded with a magnificent display of costumes and hidden faces.

Henry felt as though he would suffocate beneath the clay full-face mask. Intricate Venetian swirls lined his face and silver details surrounded the eye pieces. As he moved through the crowd, his cotton yellow sleeves brushed against passersby. He breathed in the stench of his bitter body odour and sweat itched every crevice of him. Beauty definitely came with its consequences.

Henry and Urian lifted the masks and raised the gin to their lips. The pleasant liquor dribbled into their mouths. Henry examined Urian's attire; the white blouse was concealed by a black cloth coat and red shoes. He began to wobble as he embraced the drunken embrace of the gin.

Henry looked over the crowd, for the first time, he was not an outcast. Despite his sinful plan to save Emery, nobody knew who he was beneath the fashionable attire. He was equal, they all were. He walked with pride and his heavy coat trailed at his knees. Nobody knew he was born to a low-class family where the food quality was poor and the house reeked of tallow candles or the horse dung that was stuck beneath his fingernails. Nothing mattered that night, everyone was disguised. Henry swung back the gin, a taste he couldn't get enough of. As he sipped on his beverage, the parade of feathers around his shoulders tickled his face and he couldn't help but grin.

Amongst the laughter and endless conversations, jester bells jingled through the air. The bells rang louder as a nearby crowd began to dance to the orchestral music. The conductor's hands moved swiftly above his head and the scambouche mask shielded his face. The nose was exaggeratedly long and crimson feathers flicked through the air.

"Brother, I need some more gin," Urian said.

"No, wait, wait."

Henry watched a lady hold onto the elbow of a man much taller than her. She wore a laced white dress and her blonde hair was pinned back into a wonderful bundle of curls. As she turned, her pale skin looked soft to the touch. Elongated violet feathers lined her mask which she held it up by a golden handle. She watched Henry from over her shoulder and bowed before she redirected her attention back to the orchestra.

"Well, what are you waiting for?" Urian asked.

Henry glanced up at the sky, the moon was almost directly above him. "I need to go, Emery will be waiting."

"Nonsense, the lady awaits a dance," Urian encouraged.

"There is no time left," Henry muttered.

"Of course there is. There's always time for a dance."

Urian pinched Henry's elbow and they walked forward. Henry encircled the lady and offered his hand. She accepted and her fingers were like angels'. He led the way. He twirled the lady with his hands around his waist. She moved fluidly and her pleated dress tossed in the night wind. Her grace was a pleasant embrace and one Henry wanted to pursue. He leant forward and got lost in her eyes. Then he remembered Emery and gulped against the lump in his throat. Henry had to remain focused. If he became distracted, he could risk losing Emery, for good.

"I am here with my Father, it appears as though he is watching us," the lady said in a clear voice.

"He is judging my dancing. I expect nothing less."

"He is and I think that so far, he is impressed."

Henry watched the blue eyes that glistened like a river, from behind the mask. A pendant of pearls was draped around her neck and were almost as pale as her doll-like skin. He guided the lady into his other hand and the feathers around her face blew with ease. She was one of the high-class ladies and if she saw Henry without the mask, she would never agree to a dance.So, he enjoyed it for now.

"You never told me your name."

"Mary."

Before Henry could speak, Urian danced beside them with a woman of his own. He moved faster than Henry and his jagged movements shielded her body from the rest of the crowd.

Henry looked over at him. "It's time to leave."

"Leave? What kind of gentlemen would leave such beautiful treasures all alone?" Urian asked.

His dance partner giggled. Her muslin dress was cuffed around her plump waist and she waved a fan in her free hand. Henry watched the moonlight reflect off her forehead. Time was running out, he had to start moving. "We need to go," he urged.

Suddenly Urian slipped his hands around Mary's waist

and stole the dance. The twins exchanged partners and now Henry held onto the waist of the plumper lady. She fanned herself and sent a breeze of musty sweat into Henry's face. He was partially thankful that the mask concealed the smell. He circled his dance partner. "What are you doing, Urian?"

"I can't let you leave," he whispered.

"What are you talking about? You're coming with me, aren't you?"

Urian's dance slowed and he waltzed around Mary. "I can't let you take Emery. I intend to marry Emeline and if this ordeal comes to light, her father would deny her hand in marriage. I won't be tied to the shame you will bring to the family."

"You coward, you lied to me."

"I am doing it for your own good. Now listen,I could get to Emery first and stopped your entire plan but I won't. My twin, I can see it in your eyes. The fear, the despair. I am giving you a chance to abort this plan and let Emery be taken away. I know you will do what is right. I have heard you think of it." Urian tapped his temple. "I have the other half of your mind, I can hear your thoughts. End this madness tonight."

Henry's heart pounded in his mouth. His twin betrayed him, how could he? Urian danced with Mary as if nothing happened. The crowd moved in tune to the orchestra and although their faces were covered, they appeared to enjoy themselves. They were oblivious to the disagreement between the twins. They're cluelessness was good timing.

"I'm sorry." Henry released the hand of his dance partner and walked backwards. He swallowed the bile in his mouth and it scorched his throat with fury. He turned around and ran.

*How can Urian betray me like this? He knows what I am feeling more than anyone. He knows the pain of losing our little sister and yet here we are. At a crossroad manifested from disagreement. We are so similar yet different at the same time.*

As Henry pushed through the crowd people swore at him and others stumbled aside, tripping over their dance partners. He glanced over his shoulder to see Urian was close behind. Henry panted beneath the ceramic mask. He could hardly breathe and felt as though he would faint. He couldn't remove the mask, his face would be revealed and that would draw attention to himself. The orchestra drowned out the trampling feet and annoyed remarks.

Urian ran close behind Henry and he cut through the crowd. He was a backstabber and the last person Henry suspected. He had no heart, no emotion for Emery. He was just like Father and would rather let her suffer for eternity in the asylum.

Henry rounded the water fountain; where narrow streams of water came out of angel mouths and their bodies were made of concrete that had chipped away over the years. He crouched beside it and held his breath. Up ahead was the entrance to the pleasure gardens, it was only ten feet away. Children played nearby and their beady eyes followed him.

"Look away. Look over there," Henry pointed to the crowd.

He pressed a finger to the lips of his mask, to silence the children and they nodded their heads in agreement. One of them walked towards him and Henry held up his hand. He had to think fast. "My brother and I are playing hide and seek. I need you to be quiet."

"Your brother has a nicer mask, I want him to win," one of the young girls said.

Henry shrunk into himself. "If you help me win, then we all win."

Urian slowed down as he neared the fountain. He gazed his eyes over the gardens. His fists clenched and unclenched. He stepped forward. Urian's muddy boot was right beside Henry's hand now. Urian's shoes crunched over the dirt ground, where the dust lifted and swept over Henry's face. He shut his eyes but the dust was lodged inside and began to tear up. His eyes stung as if sand was being raked over them.

Urian turned around and ran off into the gardens, he made a sharp left and disappeared from sight. Henry jumped out from his hiding spot and ran into the darkness. The children clapped and cheered, they won the game and so did Henry.

# Chapter Four

————————————-

## Before Sunrise

In the dark, Henry ran across the open fields. He ripped the mask off his face and threw it into the dirt as he leapt over fallen branches and rocks. He punched through the air but, without any source of light, he ran blindly. His throat began to tighten and he gasped for air but there was no slowing down. He had to keep moving.

Moonlight shone from the horse's trough and Henry reached forward. He pushed against the fence and threw himself into the paddock. The horses reared up on their hind legs.

"Shh, easy, easy," he uttered.

Suddenly, something moved from nearby. Henry looked around and in the far distance there was a speckle of orange light. He squinted through the darkness and the light seemed to move from side to side. Shivers descended down his spine. It looked like a lamp but Henry wasn't going to wait and find out. He turned to the bridle. No, there was not enough time.

He grabbed the elk knots along Ginny's mane, who whinnied as he pulled himself atop her back. He slammed his boot against the horse's abdomen. Ginny reared up and gravity threatened to pull Henry down but he leaned forward. He kicked Ginny again and they charged toward the fence and jumped over the paddock. Ginny bounded across the farmland and Henry pulled her mane rightward, toward the house.

The moon would be the only witness for what was about to happen. He glanced over his shoulder to see the orange light had grown nearer. Henry dug his heel into Ginny and she shot forward. He bounced with each gallop and planted his face beside her neck. The cold night sent goosebumps down his arms and pockets of wind filled his jacket, which made it an uncomfortable ride.

Henry climbed down from the horse's back and bolted inside the house. It was pitch black and there was no time to light a candle. He felt along the walls and gagged on the musty air. The bucket of urine had not been emptied yet. Henry stumbled down the hallway and relied on his memory to find the cellar. He shuffled his feet and his clammy hands fumbled across the wooden walls. At some point the rug rumpled up and

Henry tripped over it. He collided into the floor and the blisters of his hands exploded by the carpet burn. He clenched his jaw and balled his fists but the pain escalated. He was forced to plant his hands over the ground and push himself up. The sting radiated down his bones and his hands wept with pus.

"Emery! I'm coming," he called.

He reached forward, to where the cellar door should have been but it wasn't and he felt along the wall. His fingers shook uncontrollably. Without being able to see, his senses were diminished. "Where are you?"

"I'm down here," she yelled.

It came from the left. Henry pressed his body against the wall and trailed his fingers along it. He felt a bulge. It pressed against his belly. It was a doorknob. He twisted the knob, as his hands bled out. The door creaked open. "Hurry, we don't have much time."

Footsteps scuffled and a pale light moved through the cellar. It brightened only the tip of her nose. She now stood beside Henry in the doorway. The wick of the lamp was almost gone and Emery cradled the light with her hands. She shielded it from the wind as if it was her last strand of hope.

"You came back for me," she cried.

"I told you I would, did you doubt me?"

"A little bit. It would be easier for you to let me go to the asylum, the voices told me so but I never believed them. I tried not to."

Henry laid a hand on her cheek. "I'm here for you, like I promised. Are you ready to leave?"

"More than ever. I haven't stepped foot outside the cellar for almost a year," she sniffled.

Henry took the lamp and illuminated the corridor and Emery stumbled over his feet. She held onto his waist, desperate not to let go.

As they reached the front door Henry cradled the lamp with his body. A gust of wind blew and the candle light wavered. He twisted himself so his back blocked the cold and he walked towards the horse. He slipped his sore hands around Emery's waist and pushed her halfway up Ginny. Emery slipped her legs over then she looked up.

"Henry," she said. "Someone is coming."

He turned around to see the lamp was closer and there were two people running towards them.

"Give me your hand," Emery wailed.

Henry grabbed her fragile hand in one hand and Ginny's mane with the other. He hauled himself up and held onto the elk knots, securing them both atop her back. Henry raised his foot and slammed it down into the horse. Ginny charged forward, with each gallop Henry's hands ached with pain. He tightened his grasp and felt Emery's bony body beside him. She smelt of ammonia and her greasy hair was plastered against his cheek.

The pair rode off into the night, not quite sure where they were headed but as far away as possible. A wail sounded in the distance, it was their Mother. Henry's heart chipped away, as he listened to the broken cry. Mother screamed but the words got lost in the wind and it was probably for the better.

Neither of them spoke, there was nothing to say but it was in the silence that Henry began to doubt his decision.

*The night is dark as is the road ahead. I can't see any light, for there is none. There was always a light of hope for Emery and there always will be. I won't give up on her but where do I go from here? How do I restore her? I am lost. Lord, help me.*

He wasn't sure what he was doing or how to cure his sister but their bond would see them through.

Emery's head dropped forward. Her breathing grew heavy and she slipped into a light sleep, fatigue got the best of her. The night was long and despite the burn behind Henry's eyes, sleep was the last thing he thought about.

After a few minutes Ginny grew tired and slowed to a trott. Henry glanced upright at the moon that glimmered in the sky. It followed them through the unknown land and for some reason it was comforting, almost as if the moon was a guardian of the night, a guide through the mysterious woods. His eyes stung and he switched his gaze back to the land. They were immersed in a forest, where trees huddled together and Ginny was forced to change her route along the narrow path. Ginny walked around the trees and Henry's boot occasionally got snagged on the trunks, where he raked away bark. He shivered against the August night winds but Emery seemed too fatigued to notice it. She snored and her body was still. Her neck was extended forward and would probably be sore in the morning but that was the least of Henry's concerns. His eyes prickled with bitter tears. Without Urian, he was on the journey alone. He was the eldest and would be forced to lead them through the darkness. Although he had no idea where to begin, he decided the journey started the moment he stole Emery from the house. She was safe and nothing else mattered.

The forest cleared and Ginny now strode through open land. It was strange, the air was clean. Henry flared his nostrils and inhaled the pure the scent of soil, bark and dust. It was wholesome and nothing compared to the urine and ammonia that circled the York streets, especially at night. He could definitely get used to this.

Henry was too preoccupied with the questions that clouded his mind, that he didn't realise the sun rose. He cackled to himself. The sun. He did it, They made it before sunrise. He grinned to himself. His eyes slipped shut and somewhat slept beneath the dawning sun.

# Chapter Five

————————————-

## The Cleansing Stream

Emery pressed her bony shoulders against Henry's chest. He was forced awake and blinked away the morning blur. The day was young and Ginny had stopped walking. She stood beside a stream and lowered her head, to gulp mouthfuls of water. Henry climbed down and helped Emery onto the ground. Her fragile skin was covered in scratches and bruises from all the sleepless nights in the cellar. Behind the rotten-toothed smile was an innocent soul that was desperate for help. She wanted to get better but needed guidance. Henry didn't have to ask, he could just see it within her.

Emery twisted her long hair between her fingers and glared at the mattered ends that were held together by grease. Breadcrumbs were sprinkled throughout and the knots in her hair that reached down to her waist. She smelt worse than grime.

"I think I could do with a bath," she whispered and her cheeks flushed bright red.

"Me too. You get started, I have an idea."

Henry watched Emery dip her toes in the stream. She closed her eyes and tilted her head backwards. Judging by the grin on her face, she hadn't felt the embrace of water for a long time, not even a cloth to wash her face. Emery was dehumanized.

Henry walked around the land, where the grass was burnt, except for the patches of green shrubs that were protected by tree canopies. He caught sight of a twig and reached down when something caught his eyes. Behind the tree something moved. Henry stood still and a pair of floppy ears emerged. A hare bounced into sight and it looked like a ball of cotton, with two beady eyes. It sniffed the air before it hopped away. It's padded feet kicked at a twig, it would do. Henry checked over the twig in hand and walked towards the stream.

Emery was crouched into the water; her feet were planted into the dirt, her hands trailed along the surface and her dress swayed in the water. She cupped her hands, filled them with water, and cleaned her face. Her lips slipped open to exhale a heavy breath, the water was refreshing.

Henry planted his feet on either side of Emery. He looked from the stick and then back to her hair, he had never done this before. He grabbed a handful of wet hair and raked a twig through it.

"Ouch," Emery moaned.

"Sorry, I've never combed a girl's hair before."

"Start at the ends."

Henry fingered the stick through her hair, working from the bottom up. He picked at the ball of knots until the hairs loosened. After some time the knot broke free and Henry smirked at the small victory. They both worked to break away the knots and as they did, fragments of the cellar fell away. Emery's hair swirled in the river and grew in size as the knots were freed. Henry worked on the task at hand until his soggy fingers ached and the weeping blisters washed away.

"We should get a move on," he said.

"Where are we going?"

A cluster of clouds shielded pockets of blue sky and a cool breeze set in. If it rained they would be stuck without shelter. He shivered in the river, their clothes wouldn't dry any time soon and there were no spares. He didn't have the answers but he swallowed the uncertainty. Henry inserted his fingers between the strands of slimy hair and rubbed at another tight knot.

"We will sleep here for tonight and keep moving in the morning."

The dangling leaves formed a halo around Henry and Emery. They peered at the night sky from between the willow tree branches and listened to the rustle of a nearby squirrel. A tree trunk pressed against their backs but they ignored the ache. A mulberry exploded in Henry's mouth and the sweet juice dribbled down his throat. He smacked his lips together and savoured the moment. His hands scuffled around his lap, in search of another, but all that remained was their purple stains on his coat. Emery dangled a mulberry from the branch above, to which Henry accepted the offer.

He rearranged himself and swung his legs from the branch, watching the speckle of stars from beneath the tree canopy. He sighed and switched his gaze to the ground, where Ginny was tied to the tree. She grazed and tugged on the reins around her muzzle.

Emery's hands moved as if she was talking but no words were formed. She shook her head and pointed.

"I am going to throw away the rest of these mulberries." She outstretched a balled fist and opened her fingers.

The purple fruit gravitated towards the ground when Henry lunged forward and saved a few. He opened his hand to see the mulberries had spluttered in his grasp. His skin was now dyed purple and he licked the remains from his fingertips.

"No! Stop it!" Emery yelled. Her head hung upside down and she reached toward Henry, her fingers grabbed the air. "Stop eating them."

"What is the matter?"

"The berries are poisoned, you're going to die. This would never have happened if you just listened to me in the first place," she wailed.

"They are fresh mulberries, they are not harmful. Where would you get an idea like that?"

Emery sat upright and her feet hung beside Henry's face. "You don't believe me and now I will be responsible for your death."

"Have you been talking to the voices again?"

"No."

"Don't lie to me. I know you too well for that. One moment you're normal and the next you're like this. It makes no sense, Emery. There are no voices. Look around, do you see anyone?"

"Yes."

Emery folded her arms and spoke to the invisible voices. she whispered faster and hints of the foreign tongue slipped into the conversation. Henry climbed onto the branch above. He clasped both hands over her ears and locked his eyes on hers. She bit into her nail bed and continued talking to the voices over Henry's shoulder. A glimmer of fear shot across her eyes and her nostrils flared. Emery's teeth clamped into her lower lip and show-cased the fragments of mulberry were lodged in her gums. Henry pressed his nose against hers and remained silent. He stared at her until his eyes stung. His thumb felt the throbbing pulse from the veins beside her temple. He remained calm and breathed slowly.

The hopeless eyes of Emery locked sight onto his lips. Henry's breathing was paced and she mirrored the same. A single tear trickled down her cheek and he wiped it away. She nodded, curled up on the branch and shut her eyes. The voices disappeared.

"Get some sleep. I'll be on the branch below," Henry said.

Atop the bony branch Henry coiled into a foetal position with his arms wrapped around the branch. His head throbbed with the events of the day, too much had happened. He wanted to forget it all but the cold breeze was a constant reminder that he was far from home. The bark was his pillow and the river ripples were the song that lulled him to sleep. Henry shut his eyes but they burned from the inside out. The blackness behind his eyelids was anything but comforting. He had no idea where he was and had never travelled so far from home. He shivered. All he could think about was a blanket. A single leaf planted itself over Henry's waist. The leaf was his blanket in the wilderness and he slipped into sleep.

# Chapter Six

————————————-

## Wilderness

Ginny and Henry walked across the landscape which was almost flat and nothing like the farmland back home. They travelled along an invisible path and made up the turns they took. Henry's clothes were damp and the silk leggings itched his legs all over.

Atop the horse was Emery. She sat in silence and glanced over the terrain. Her feet dangled over the side as she twirled her fingers. "Why am I like this?"

"You can't help it," Henry mumbled. "I know your mind is tainted and I understand that but why did you speak to the voices? You should have ignored them. You knew better."

"They were going to hurt someone if I didn't talk back."

"Who would that be?"

"You."

Henry halted. His heart beat within his skull and his face crumpled into a frown.

Emery toyed with her gown. "What do you mean when you say that you understand why my mind is like this?"

"At the time I thought the doctor was a quack. I thought a curse had been cast upon you but now I can see that I was wrong to dismiss him. He knows more than I do."

"What did he say?"

"You were in the room, don't you remember?"

Henry glanced over his shoulder to see Emery's mouth drop open. A thousand questions were scribbled across her face. A single tear trickled down her pale cheek. Emery's lips moved but she didn't speak and the brown eyes were glum. A shadow cast over her solemn face, his question was answered.

"The doctor examined you in the cellar, it was around the time the voices started. He said the reason most women become insane is because of their organs. It is the female womb that manifests these dark desires. It pushes you away from faith and whispers in your ear. At the time I thought he was wrong, that it was a demon's work, just like the priest said. Now, I am not so sure. The female womb causing this problem was a new concept for me to digest but it all makes sense now. You have to fight it, Emery."

"I don't know how."

"Neither do I but we shall find a way."

"What did the doctor recommend?"

"A bleed, purge, leech therapy, fresh air. Father dismissed the conversation early and listened to the priest instead. Who recommended ..."

Emery gasped. "You mean the York -"

"Shh!" Henry cut her off. "Yes, now, don't say the name."

Henry couldn't fathom the thought of never seeing his sister again. The tales of the asylum involuntarily flooded back into his mind; screams that echoed down the hallways, the medications shoved down patients throats and the endless urge to walk freely.

Henry's head thumped and his stomach gurgled. They couldn't live off berries for much longer. In the distance was endless green terrain and not a house in sight. He stared at his feet and trudged through the shrubbery, a change of clothes would be desirable. His big toe now protruded out of the shoe. Great. As if the journey couldn't get any more uncomfortable.

He lifted his gaze and from the corner of his eye he saw what appeared to be a brown boulder. That was strange. He stopped walking and focused. He realised it was a moose with a calf beside it. The grazing moose looked over at the intruders. Clipped pieces of grass clung to her proboscis as she chewed the remains. She turned to the calf, who was covered in a layer of fuzzy fur and the button eyes.

Henry clenched his grip around the reins and walked backwards but Ginny didn't move. She simply stared at the moose. He jabbed his elbow into her neck. The next few moves had to be slow, the last thing he wanted was to disrupt the moose. He tugged on the saddle and began to haul himself atop Ginny. The odd but familiar rotten stench of ammonia lifted through the air. That couldn't be. There was no town or people nearby.

Suddenly, an ear-piercing snap broke through the forest.

Again.

Bam.

Gunshots. The moose and calf trampled into the distance. Their heavy hooves vibrated through the ground.

"Keep your head down!" Henry roared.

Emery clutched her head and closed her eyes. Gunshots flew from all directions. They ricocheted off nearby trees and kicked up the dirt ground. Henry couldn't make sense of which direction they came from. Ginny trampled her hooves and neighed loudly. She shook her head and the bridle swayed. Another round of gunshots rang through the air and dirt exploded around the horse.

Ginny reared up on her hind legs and kicked the air. Henry pulled the reins but the straps burned his blistered hands. Suddenly, Emery lost her balance. She topped over the horse and collided into the ground.

But she was quick to get back on her feet and grabbed Henry's hand. He began to haul her up when a force tugged her away. The skinny fingers slipped from his grasp. A greyhound now barked in Emery's face. Its white body poised on-top of her body and saliva dribbled into her mouth. It was muddled and about her size.

Henry leapt down, grabbed the hound by the neck and pulled it away. It kicked its scrawny legs and snapped its jaws. Henry locked the dog in his arms and the canine teeth chomped beside his face.

Running feet sounded from somewhere near. Henry looked around and in the distance was a pair of hunters. They slowed down and soon made sense of the scene. One dropped down besides Emery and peeled her hands away from her ears. He laid a hand on her back and searched around. The other hunter pointed the rifle at Henry. He watched him from the sight of the gun.

"Put the dog down," the older voice said.

"I am not hurting him but this mutt attacked my sister."

The hunter straightened the gun, which was now pointed between Henry's eyes. He had no choice but to listen to the stranger. He let go of the dog's neck and the hunter whistled. The hound leapt over and stood at his heels.

"She's not hurt," the other one said. "What are you doing in the woods? You could've gotten killed."

"Well that was obviously not our intention." Henry tilted his hat. "Now, if you'll excuse us. We must be on our way."

"The moose is lost because of you fools."

"Right, then, I better retrieve it for you."

One of the hunters patted down his pockets. "My knife is gone too." He glared at Henry.

"Don't look at me, I don't have it. I was too busy fighting your mutt."

"It's my grandfather's knife. Let's go then, I just have dropped it somewhere."

Henry stared at the strangers, who retraced their steps. The hound bared its teeth and stared at Emery. The fur on his back stood on end.

"Come," the hunter said.

The hound remained still. The hunter whistled and it slowly turned around.

A strange feeling surged within Henry's stomach. He turned around to see Emery's eyes were locked on the dog. Her brown-stained teeth protruded as he spoke. The sound of bubbling saliva emitted from her mouth along with the foreign whispers. Her bloodshot eyes didn't blink, she appeared as though she was in another reality.

# Chapter Seven

------------------

## In a Nutshell

Beneath the walnut tree, the cracked nut shells were tossed to the ground. Henry pressed his back against Ginny and offered her one. A pile of about ten empty nutshells were beside Henry's foot. He reached up and pulled another one off the branch. He offered it to Emery who refused the dinner.

"You have to eat something," Henry encouraged. He smashed the walnut shell against a rock and removed the shards of shell. "You haven't eaten properly for almost two days, enough of this."

"Father would punish me the same way. What's the difference between then and now?"

Henry leaned in. "I'm here now. Besides, I brought you food all the time."

She looked over the peeled walnut and chiselled away at the edges with her teeth. The nut flesh lay inside her mouth and she leaned against the tree trunk. He sighed, she would have to swallow it at some point.

Emery looked over her shoulder. Her eyes locked on something and she no longer blinked. Her eyes searched the landscape but Henry ignored the sudden change in behaviour. He was fatigued and for the time being, not interested in the thoughts inside her head. The walnut fell to the ground and Henry ate it instead.

"Why would you want me to do that?" Emery whispered. She looked at Henry as she snuck a hand inside her dress pocket and extracted something. It looked like an iron handle. As the full body of the object was revealed, Henry realised it was a knife. The pointed edge faced his chest.

He stared at the knife and a glint of moonlight shone from the tip. Emery held it with shaking hands. The knife quivered and blood oozed from her nail beds, where she chewed on her own skin. It dribbled along the cold metal. "Why would you ask me to do this?"

"Who is asking you, Emery? Who wants you to do what?"

*She is possessed by her own body. Her womanhood has taken control of her hands. If I move, the knife will be plunged into my chest. If I stay still, I suffer the same fate as her. What shall I do? I have never seen her in*

*this state. To this degree. Maybe there is nothing else to*
*be done but simply watch. Like a coward.*

Emery fought something, or someone that couldn't be seen. She frowned and pressed the knife closer to Henry. He shuffled away, careful not to make any sudden moves.

"Emery, don't hurt me. I am your brother."

She stared at him, confused. She mouthed the word *why* over and over again. "Why are you asking me to do this?"

Ginny moved aside and Henry toppled over. He slammed into the ground and a dull ache emitted from his back. He shielded his face with his hands. Emery rambled on but the conversation was senseless. Henry dribbled, too scared to even swallow. Any movement could send a knife through his heart.

Rain trickled over them. Emery clutched her head as droplets exploded against her face.

"Stop that knocking. Tap. Tap. Tap. The rain is trying to get inside my head … Stop saying that!" Emery wailed.

"I didn't say anything."

"The voices. There's so many. I don't know which one to listen to."

"Listen to me. Follow my voice."

"I am trying! The voices sound like you, Henry. I don't know which one is really your voice. I can hear you from different directions. Why would you want me to kill you?"

"I am your brother! Stop this nonsense and listen to me. Do not kill me!" Henry stared at her. "Look at my lips. Read my words."

"I can hear your voice from all around. Your voice is the wind, your voice is the river and the sand beneath my feet. I can hear you begging to be surrendered into an eternal slumber. If this will ease your suffering brother, then I shall do it. This is for you."

Emery raised the blade above her head and Henry reached for it. The knife sliced through the air and almost severed his fingers. He cowered away and covered his face with his hands. His eyes shut and were shielded by his knuckles. Emery dropped to her knees and clutched the knife with both hands. "Forgive me."

The knife plunged forward and Henry shut his eyes. His flesh split open. Tendons were severed. Hot blood spurted out.

The knife went through the other side of Henry's hand and was pressed against his forehead. His own blood dripped down his face and the awful crimson fluid slipped into his mouth. It tasted bitter and warm.

His hand was almost torn in two. The obnoxious thump of his heart pounded inside his skull. So much so, that he was going to be sick. It was his left hand. Of course, the hand of evil. The hand which Emery has followed. Blood oozed along the sterling knife and his fingers shook uncontrollably. The pain was numbing and soon Henry was consumed with the grappling sting. It had total control.

He roared and attempted to cradle his hand, wanting to protect his wound from Emery but he couldn't bear the thought of touching it. Instead he watched his deformed hand shake and spurt with blood. Dirt crumbled as Henry's heels pressed into the ground. Veins bulged from his head whilst he screamed until his breath gave out. Emery dropped to her knees, speechless.

"Pull the damned knife out of my hand!"

Her eyes widened by what she must do. She grabbed the handle and tugged upwards. But she took Henry's hand with it. He cried and jerked away.

*Damn it! She's too weak to help me. Mortified by what she has done. How am I supposed to do this alone? Everything will be fine, once the knife is removed. It's not that bad … I'll pull it out on three.*

*One.*

*Two.*

*Three.*

Henry pulled the blade out of his hand and blood squirted into the air. He pressed his thumb into the hole of his hand and tried to compress the wound but it didn't help. His shirt was dyed crimson as were his arms. He peered up at the sky. From the dismal clouds, rain pelleted down. The droplets exploded over his hand. It felt like fire from inside. Henry clenched his jaw and dug his feet into the ground. He hunched forward, to protect his hand from the rain. He sobbed a hopeless plea into the dirt. There was nothing more he could do.

Emery grabbed the hem of her dress and tugged on it. The fabric frayed but the rain made it harder to tear. She wrapped the edge around her hand and pulled again, this time tearing off an entire piece.

"Come here," she leaned forward and draped the fabric over Henry's hand. His fingers shook, he knew what had to be done. "Do it."

She wrapped the fabric around the palm of his hand and tightened it. Hard. The pain intensified, if that were even possible. The hole in his hand was contorted from all angles. A gush of blood wept out. "Again," he wailed.

Emery looped the fabric over his hand and fastened a

knot around his knuckles. The blood mixed with the rain and evaporated into the soil. The metallic scent of blood lifted through the air, it made Henry dizzy. His hand pulsed until the pain numbed his mind.

He looked at Emery. She pleaded for mercy but at that moment, he couldn't forgive her. She tried to take his life. Henry had another idea. He reached forward and placed his bleeding hand against her cheek.

"Pray for forgiveness," Henry said.

Despite the cold from the rain, they prayed in unison. Henry mouthed the words of prayer but his mind drifted.

*I can see the burn from inside, she is hurting. Probably as much as I am but I am not willing to listen to her merciful cry. I am tired, so tired of trying to find a way to save her. I am tired of being lost and helpless. She needs a miracle. She must pray for it and maybe then, she will be changed. Maybe then, I can forgive her. Just, maybe.*

# Chapter Eight

----------------------------

## To Live in Your own Reality

A blood handprint was crusted against Ginny's flank. At some point the rain ceased and Henry awoke with a stiff neck. He peeled himself off the horse and raised his hand before the rising sun. His nails were encircled with black dirt and coarse horse hair clung to the make-shift bandage. He examined the bandage, which was no longer white but red-and-brown. The pain beat through his veins and radiated up his arm.

"I'm going to get an infection. We must find a town."

No response.

Henry rolled his eyes at the silence. He peered around, to see Emery was crouched beside a puddle of mud. Her black hair trailed in the dirt as did her bare feet. She whispered to the ground and her hands worked on something.

Henry hauled himself up and cradled the wounded hand against his abdomen. He crouched down and watched her chapped lips move rhythmically. Her eyes darted across the ground and her fingers toyed with the mud. He grabbed her wrist and held it still. He was too exhausted to ask what was going on. There was never a good reason for her actions.

She fiddled with the dirt as if no one was watching and saliva dribbled from her lips. Henry's grasp tightened around her arm. His fingers dug into her skin but she ignored him.

"That's enough. No more of this stupidity. I need to get to a doctor."

Emery giggled. She covered her mouth with her elbow and then continued fiddling with the mud. She attempted to reposition her hands but couldn't fight off Henry's grasp. Instead, she used her free hand and held a circular object before her eyes. It dripped with sticky mud and she blew against it. Speckles of soil dropped to the ground. Her thumb rubbed against the object and a light brown protruded through. It was a walnut.

"Are you listening to me?"

"You won't get sick," Emery chuckled. "I found a way to heal your wound, brother. Let me get to work, won't you?" Her eyes beamed with triumph.

Henry stared at her. Rage burned within his stomach. "Do you take me for an idiot?"

"Hush now," Emery cackled. She dug at the ground and dropped the walnut inside. With a handful of dirt, she sprinkled it into the hole and grinned. "This will heal you."

"That's a nut! What are you talking about?"

"It's the key to the prairie. It will help us."

Henry's eyes almost bulged out of his head. He couldn't believe what he heard. This was insane. Emery was further away from reality and he had no idea where to turn. He lifted her chin and stared into her eyes. They were blurry. Possessed. She changed and was no longer the innocent sister he remembered.

"You're going crazy."

"No, I'm not. She told me this would work. Now your hand shall be healed."

"Enough of that. Get on the horse."

"What?"

"I don't have time for questions. Get on the horse. Now!"

Emery did as she was told.

Henry held the reins and led them west. It should be the direction they were yesterday, when the hunters came along. He prayed they weren't far from a town. To find treatment for his hand wasn't the only reason they headed for civilization. He wasn't lying, he would lose his hand if it didn't stop bleeding soon but there was even more at stake. The both of them needed food and Emery required help. A doctor. Henry couldn't save her alone, he needed guidance. If he sought what he needed from another town, nobody would recognise them. Emery would bring no shame to the family and word of her illness would remain a secret. Just like his parents desired.

Henry's hand wept and he tried to ignore the throb from inside. Droplets of fresh blood evaporated into Ginny's fur. Her melanin coat consumed it.

He focused his kind on something else, home. His stomach turned over at the thought of home. He missed the dim Georgian house, the musty stench of tallow candles and the days spent working with Urian on the farm. Although terrible, food was guaranteed. Now, in the wilderness, there was no light.

*If I didn't know any better, I would say that Emery is getting worse. She is hallucinating more than before. Perhaps she was always this way and I never spent enough time with her to realise. She is more mad than I ever knew possible. Prayer only works so much for the spirits inside her womb, which have noe made a home. Her body is their house and they shall be cast out by a purge. A purge to heal her womb. I can't let Emery know, she would never agree to it but it's for the best. I know it. Faith is the only way out.*

A tear trickled down his cheek. *Is there even a town in this direction?*

"Henry, I'm hungry," Emily broke the silence.

"I tried to get you to eat but you didn't listen."

"That food was poisoned, maybe we can get something from the town?"

Henry reached inside his pocket. He had a few shillings. It would be just enough for a loaf of bread and a doctor.

"When will we know if I am healed?"

"When you act normal and stop listening to the evil spirits that whisper in your ear."

"I'm sorry," Emery twiddled her thumbs. "How much longer will this trip last?"

Henry swallowed against the lump in his throat. So far nothing had worked; isolation in the cellar, prayer, fresh air, talking sense into her. He had gotten nowhere. In the next town, he would try another purge or whatever was recommended, Emery couldn't know his plan, it could frighten her. He refused to accept defeat and end the journey any time soon because that would mean ... The York Retreat. Out of the question.

Dusk was upon the forest and Henry's hand began to throb. It pulsated with pain and tingled down his arm. He stumbled over the rocks and shrubs. Through the sunset the forest all looked the same. He no longer knew which way was west.

"There it is," Emery said.

"You're seeing things."

"No, honest. It's over there." She pointed into the distance.

Henry followed her finger and through the trees, he saw a speckle of orange light. It was too good to be true. Lanterns spread like fire embers across the streets. They moved slow and were carried by small children. He stumbled in the direction of the lanterns. He ducked beneath the tree branches and a few feet away was the over-used dirt road that zig-zagged through the town. An array of orange-panelled roofs beamed in the sunset. It looked like Scarborough.

# Chapter Nine

----------------

## Foreign Help

The bread didn't taste like forty shillings worth. Even so, they forced it down their throats. Henry lubricated the bread with saliva and choked on the crumbs. His stomach turned over, it was hardly enough but it would keep him alive. He searched Scarborough, which was almost desolate but the stench of ammonia was stronger than York. He grabbed the handkerchief from his coat and held it over his nose; the scent of mould and soil seemed better.

"Move aside!" A grumpy voice called.

Henry peered around to see an elderly man headed in his direction. He rode a horse-led carriage and scoffed at them. A saddlebag was flung over his shoulder and a thick cigar in the corner of his mouth. His black attire and polished boots seemed professional despite his stoic appearance.

"Excuse me," Henry called.

The stranger sighed and pulled the horse to a halt.

"Can you help us? We are looking for a doctor."

The man's back faced them but from around the side of his face a trail of smoke lifted through the air. He blew out another mouthful of cigar smoke. "That depends on what you need help with. I am a doctor but have just finished my duties for today."

"Please sir, my hand is seriously wounded. I have been stabbed."

"You need a dispensary, the doctors there can give you medicine."

"No. It just needs to be re-bandaged."

The doctor sighed. "Follow me."

The doctor showed them down a narrow alleyway. Ginny almost couldn't fit through, much less turn around. The bricked walls reached sky high and rats scattered across the dirt ground. Their vermin feet scratched the walls and disappeared inside crevices. Ginny jerked backward as Henry covered her eyes.

The alley widened and they now walked along the rear-end of wooden houses. Henry pinched the handkerchief around his nose but the ammonia still crept in. The doctor dismounted from the horse and was no taller than five-foot-five. His black coat trailed at his ankles. Wiry gray hair hung below his shoulders, his face was covered with deep wrinkles and his eyelids sagged, half-closed. The doctor held onto a walking stick and rounded the brown horse. He walked towards a domed door of the wooden cottage. He looked over at Henry.

"Are you coming?"

The house was crammed with vases, ornaments and stacks of textbooks. The doctor pushed the clutter aside by the end of his walking stick and ventured towards the drawing room. Henry felt Emery's sweaty fingers hold his own as she walked close behind and commonly stepped on his feet. Her warm breath blew against his neck and then he realised, this was her first time in another town. He glanced over his shoulder, the door was ajar and Ginny was tied to a lamp post.

In the drawing room they squashed into the beige couch. Henry was in the middle and his knees were pressed beside Emery's bony legs. The doctor pulled up a stool and opened his hand. Henry scrounged around his pocket and gave him a few shillings. It was all he had left. The doctor raised an eyebrow.

"Let me have a look at your hand."

Henry offered his left hand and the doctor snipped the

fabric open with metal scissors. The makeshift-bandage unravelled and fell to the floor. The awful scent of flesh filled the room and his hand shook. The doctor examined the stab wound and as he moved Henry's hand, it wept. He clenched his jaw and groaned.

"I have alcohol I can give you but you will need a dispensary to stitch this up."

"I can do without the dispensary."

The doctor stared at Henry. His mouth slipped open to speak but he said nothing and an aroma of his acidic breath emitted from between his yellow-stained teeth. The doctor rummaged around the far corner of the drawing room. He opened the doors of the cabinet and extracted a few supplies.

Henry turned to Emery. She was confused and searched his face for answers that never came.

*I trust this man, his words speak truthfully. If he was lying about being a doctor, I would know. My faith in the divine would lead us away from harm, I know this is true. We could never go to a dispensary. There are too many professionals there. They would find out about Emery's illness and the word would be out for all of Britain to know. Then, I would never see her again. She could be prosecuted and sent to the lunatic asylum. This doctor is our only hope of helping us and keeping her illness a secret. Whatever he recommends, I will do. Whatever happens now, is for the better.*

The doctor doused Henry's hand in alcohol, which stung from inside out. Then, without warning, he slipped the needle into his skin. Henry cried out as the hook broke through the other side of his flesh. The doctor continued to sew his hand together with a straight face. The task felt as though it took hours and the pain intensified.

He looked over at Emery, who clasped her hands over her ears. Henry screamed inside his mouth, his cheeks blew up with air. His wails were drowned out and Emery slowly removed her hands.

"I haven't seen either of you around here before," the doctor said. He was so close to Henry's hand that his nose almost touched it.

"We are from afar."

"From the prair-" Emery began but silenced when Henry jabbed her abdomen.

"What are you doing here?"

"I am on a quest for answers. Perhaps you could help me?"

The doctor raised an eyebrow and paused the rhythmical movements of his hands. He watched Henry from the corner of his eyes. Then he looped the needle through the open flesh again.

"My sister needs help. Her mind is ill."

Henry clenched his jaw as a fresh bandage was wrapped around his hand.

The doctor remained silent and when the dressing was complete he leaned back into the chair. "I can attempt a bleed but it will cost you."

"I don't have any more shillings."

"Very well, then my hands are tied." The doctor grinned and the wrinkles of his cheeks crumpled.

"Please help me. I know I don't have much to offer but I am desperate. My sister will go to an asylum if I cannot find a cure," Henry pleaded.

"If you cannot pay then I cannot help you. What would you like me to possibly do?"

Henry thought in silence. Time hung by a thread, for they had no clean clothes, money or food. They would need to return home soon and Henry's mission was far from accomplished. Father would be more disappointed than he could imagine. He stole Emery and would return her the way she was. Worse even. He would bring the family so much shame, they would be the talk of the town.

"Show me what to do. Tell me how to help my sister and I will follow your lead."

"I don't normally do this." The doctor grabbed a piece of paper and scribbled on it. After some time he handed it to Henry. "I shouldn't be the one giving this to you but if I remember correctly, this is how to perform a purge. Don't tell anyone I gave you this. Now leave."

Henry knew not to ask any questions. He looked at his freshly bandaged hand and an ache pulsed through his fingers. The pain was jaw-clenching but he couldn't afford medications. His shaking fingers looked over the written page. The letter read like a prayer, one that would cast out the possession and bring back the lost soul. They needed candles and a priest. Henry's stomach sank for a moment but he figured his faith would have to be enough. He would do the honours and save Emery himself. He folded the letter.

"Come on, it's time to go," Henry said.

A tear fell from Emery's eye. The fear was palpable. It seemed a part of her didn't want to get better. Or maybe she was scared of what that meant. Henry gulped, what else could he do?

The semi-crescent moon shadowed Henry. It followed them through the woods. It reminded him of home, of the night light that glistened through the bedside curtains and all the evenings that he star-gazed with Urian.

*It's just a thought and I'm probably going mad but I feel only half-alive. Here, in the wilderness, I am only half of who I am. Urian is nowhere near. I have never felt this way before. We've always been conjoined at the umbilical cord, never alone. I miss being able to read his thoughts or feel whatever he did.* Henry sighed. *I don't know where to go from here. I am no priest, how can I perform this purge? Maybe I am looking in all the wrong areas and need to turn towards the cathedral. I need a holy man. I need my twin. I need answers. What would he do at a time like this? More-so, what should I do? Without my brother, I only have half of the answers I need.*

Henry felt Emery's scrawny fingers toy with the edge of his coat. She tugged on the fabric and picked at the stitch-line. The vibrations through the coat irritated him but he was too fatigued to attest.

"I am sorry for your hand," Emery said.

"I'm alright."

"It wasn't me. I didn't do it, the voices did."

"No, you did this."

"You don't believe me." Emery pinched the thread until it ripped. "The voices are not inside my head, they are all around me. I hear them all the time and I have to stop myself from speaking to them. You would never understand."

"After this purge they will disappear and you will be redeemed. I know everything will be okay. You just wait and see."

"I don't want to do it!" Emery wailed at the top of her lungs.

Henry turned around and clasped his hands around her mouth. "Shh, shh," he calmed her down. Her muffled voice emitted and her lips pressed against his fingers. "Someone will hear you."

Emery raised her hand and slapped Henry across the face. His cheek burned and his grip loosened. It caught him off guard. Before he could do anything, Emery tumbled off the horse. She fell to the ground and leapt to her feet. She spoke in a foreign tongue and Henry caught her eye. Her face was still but her lips moved. The words tumbled out as she spoke faster. She ran off into the distance. Her hands punched through the air and darkness engulfed her. Henry kicked Ginny and she ran after her. Then, the sound of her voice weakened. She headed in the other direction.

Just up ahead was the meek figure of Emery. Henry bounced atop Ginny's back and reached forward. His fingers slipped through Emery's hair. She ran, all the while, yelling at the top of her lungs. She spat into the air, talking to the voices. The words, that sounded Latin, rolled off her tongue. Henry leant forward again and then she dropped to the ground.

Ginny dodged the fallen body and slipped aside. She whinied and skidded across the ground. Henry was thrown off her back. His head smeared into the soil and he flopped on-top of his wounded hand. He roared in agony.

Ginny tried to sit upright. Her hooves kicked the dirt and she panicked the more she struggled to manoeuvre herself. Henry patted her flank and then pressed his shoulder into her. He pushed with all of his might. Ginny sat upright for a brief moment but she soon collapsed.

Henry noticed wood chippings were strewn across the grass. That was odd. He turned around to see a pair of wooden doors loomed a few feet away. Emery ran straight inside. Towards a faint light that glowed. It seeped from beneath a pair of wooden doors. It was a barn.

# Chapter Ten

————————————-

## Upon A Stranger's Land

The stone walls were lined with farm tools and the floor was covered in hay. It crunched beneath their boots. The pitched roof was held up by log beams and there was the revolting stench of faeces. Most likely from sheep. Henry's bones warmed from the inside out, although the wind howled from the doorway. He looked outside, where he had tied Ginny to a tree. Her leg was fractured and she wouldn't be able to manoeuvre herself inside. She shall sleep there tonight. The whale oil from a lamp evaporated the oxygen from the room and replaced it with the musty stench of fish and sea salt. Even so, Henry cradled the lamp and felt the warmth weep inside his wound.

Emery sat on the floor and bunched up the straw, until it somewhat resembled a pillow, and she sank her head into it. She brought her legs to her chest and tucked her feet beneath her dress. Her eyes slipped shut but she nibbled along her nail beds.

"I don't believe it," Henry said to himself. "We will leave in the morning but let me rest first."

He curled into a foetal position and placed a handful of straw over his back. The candle crackled from the doorway and the halo of light illuminated the barn. He watched the fire dance until his eyes grew tired and slipped shut.

Henry was forced awake when a blunt object poked his stomach. He wiped away the morning blur and saw a pair of petite feet now stood before him. The stumpy toes were covered in dirt and they stepped backwards. He raised his gaze and was met by the confused glare of a young boy, who aimed the stick at Henry's face and poked his cheek. The child was dressed in brown overalls and his chestnut eyes watched the strangers beneath a thick bed of blonde hair.

Henry sat upright and stared at the boy. They remained silent, each of them equally suspicious of each other's presence.

"What is your name?" Henry asked.

"Little John," the squeaky voice replied.

That was an odd way to be addressed. Henry almost laughed but held a stern face. He was only a boy after all. "Well then, Little John, what exactly are you doing in this barn?"

"This is my father's barn. Why are you here?"

"I needed somewhere to sleep. It is very cold outside and my sister is not well. She is in desperate need of some rest. Do you think we could stay here for a short while? Just until she is well enough to get on her feet."

"What happened to your hand?" Little John raised the stick to Henry's injured hand. The once fresh bandages were now blood stained and the hay was dyed red. The stitches were probably ripped open. He hung his head, how would he explain to the boy what had happened? He would be petrified of Emery.

"Would you be able to fetch us some fresh water and bread? My sister and I have not eaten in many days."

Little John nodded and darted outside the barn.

Henry lighty tread across the barn, he walked slow, careful now to wake Emery. He stood in the barn entrance, where the lamp light was replaced by a trail of smoke. The warm sun chased away the shadows from the barn. Henry stood in the doorway and the sight was intriguing. Open landscapes of endless hills and sheep were before him. Animals grazed and horses galloped in the next paddock. It felt like home. His eyes locked on

Ginny, who was half-hidden by the overgrown weeds as she gnawed on the shrubs. Henry ventured outside and crouched down to stroke her mane. Then he grabbed her front hoof, which was extended forward at an awkward angle. Ginny whinnied and moved uncomfortably.

"Alright, alright, I think it's broken," Henry sighed. "My friend, you won't be able to journey much further. It ends here."

Henry pulled out a handful of grass and laid it before Ginny. Her thick lips protrude forward and munched loudly only on the fresh trimmings. He turned around and headed towards the barn, where Little John now sat on a pile of hay.

There was a plate of fresh bread and Henry bit off more than he could swallow. He forced the breakfast down his dry throat. He raised the cup to his lips where water trickled into his mouth and dampened the bread. Emery cupped her hands and inhaled the bread. She hardly swallowed and gulped down the water. It was nice to see her finally eat.

"Why did you come here?" Little John asked as he toyed with a fragment of bark. He must have only been about six years old and far too young to understand the journey Henry and Emery had been on. "We were out riding when the storm struck and my horse, Ginny, right there, she ran the wrong way. Stupid animal, she only listens sometimes."

Little John giggled. "You need to train her, I could do it for you. My father says I am going to be the best horse rider when I am older. I can show you how to train her!" His eyes beamed with triumph and a gummy smile was etched across his face.

"Maybe one day," Emery agreed.

A whistle sounded from nearby. Little John glanced over his shoulder and dropped the bark to the ground. "Mama is calling me, I better go. Will you be here tonight? I do not have any brothers or sisters. I do get quite lonely here."

"Yes, we will be here," she said.

Little John darted out of the barn and his shadow disappeared around the corner. Henry licked the crumbs off of her fingers. He was satisfied with the breakfast but he couldn't help but think, whose farm was this?

As the day matured, Henry paced back and forth within the barn, reading the purge script the doctor had written. He memorised it, word for word. Then he tucked the paper away and gazed through the doorway. He opened his mouth to speak of the purge prayer he memorised but choked on the words. He knew none of it, for his mind was adrift with despair. Time had run out and they could not shelter in the barn for much longer. He would soon be forced to return home but Emery was not ready. She was not cured and if anything, she had deteriorated.

*I am lost, my Lord. Shed your light and guide me down this narrow path. How can I save my sister if I cannot read aloud the words to help her? There must be another way but I cannot do this alone, I need your guidance. Your grace to show me the way through the darkness. Help us before it is too late. I know I am a sinner, for salvaging a person that speaks to evil but she is good. I know it.*

The crack of wood broke through Henry's thoughts. He turned around to see Emery was no longer in sight. That was odd. She hadn't left, for he guarded the door the whole time. The creak sounded again but it came from above. He switched his gaze upright and there was Emery, walking along the beams. Her hands were outspread like wings, that guided her balance. She walked towards the wall, focused on the beam beneath her feet. A tear dribbled down her chin.

Henry's body burned with fatigue. "Emery, get down from there."

"I cannot. This is the only way out, for both you and me."

"I have the way out, see this?" Henry raised the letter in the air. "The doctor gave me the answers to help you. Once we complete the purge I will set you free."

"Was it the doctor from the prairie?"

"No, the one from Scarborough!" Henry yelled.

"I have never been to Scarborough. Is it beautiful? Are the people pleasant and doctors kind?"

Henry's jaw dropped open.

*Emery is mad, madder than mad. Her mind is deteriorating more by the day which means that I am losing time. She is delusional, living in a false reality. She is further away from sanity than I could have ever anticipated and I fear there is no hope left. I have failed but I will not lose her forever.*

Henry extended his hand. "Come down."

"There is only one way down." She tapped her temple. "I know so."

Emery switched her gaze to the roof and sunk her teeth into her lower lip. She broke open an old wound and puss seeped into her mouth. Henry guessed that the voices were nearby. Her cheeks puffed up and she held back a scream. Veins bulged from her forehead as she tried to contain every emotion that choked her.

"I'm right here," Henry pleaded.

Emery's eyes rolled into the back of her head. Her legs wobbled and she tumbled forward. She fell from the beam and her dress blew in the air. Henry leapt forward and extended his arms just in time. She fell into his grasp. Her weight forced him to the ground but at least she was safe. Although, she was not yet safe from insanity.

# Chapter Eleven

--------------- -

## A Cheap Trade-off

By nightfall Little John reappeared within a plate of sausages and potatoes. He laid it on the ground before the hungry hands. Emery dug into the dinner but Henry held back.

"I did a good job bringing the food, didn't I? Mama fell asleep too early to notice that it was gone," Little John said.

"Where is the cutlery?" Henry asked.

"Oh," Little John pressed a finger to his chin in thought. "I guess I forgot," he shrugged.

"Never mind." Henry sat on the floor and bent his knees. As he ate the sausage oil trailed along his hands which rested over his knee. He gnawed on the over-cooked sausage and the squelching sound of saliva left his mouth. Little John stared at the food, almost as if he was hungry himself.

"There is enough to share," Emery suggested.

"That is alright. Mama says I am greedy and I already

had my own dinner earlier so I don't think I should eat some more."

"You're a growing boy." She offered the other half of her sausage to Little John. He took a small bite and thought for a moment.

"I almost forgot! I have some fresh clothes for you."

Little John stuffed his hands into his pockets and almost skipped out of the barn. He soon reappeared with a handful of once-clean clothes, now stained with oily fingerprints, and dumped them on the floor. Henry reached forward and examined the button shirt, which had  frilled sleeves and pleated tunic. They exchanged their old clothes for the new ones and the bitter smell of body odour almost halved. Emery looked elegant in a navy blue dress that hung loosely from her waist and dragged across the floor.

"Thank you, Little John," Henry nodded. "You have been very hospitable but we should leave soon. Perhaps in the coming days."

"You can't leave," Little John complained. "I rarely have company and I do not have any siblings. Where are you from?"

"We come from York, on a farm much like this and I am a farmer. Although, I think your farm looks much greener." Henry crossed his legs and polished off the remainder of dinner.

"I have been to York, on a trip with my father. We sell our produce there sometimes."

The sound of jogging footsteps erupted. Henry's ears focused on the sound, someone was near. Then, a figure stood in the doorway. A man placed his hands on his hips and pulled his hat down to his brows. "Little John!" He exclaimed. "What on earth are you doing?"

"Father, I was just ... " his voice trailed off.

"I knew you were up to no good, I've been watching you come in here at odd hours. Who the hell are you two?"

Henry's stomach sank into his spine. He stood upright and tried to swallow the remains of his food but choked on it. "I am Henry Gilchrist and this is Emery Gilchrist. We got lost in the woods and stumbled upon your place. We just about to leave."

"You're not going anywhere! Not after eating my food and wearing my finest shirt!" The man pointed a scrawny finger. His front teeth were missing and face was covered in scars.

"Are you a farmer?" Henry asked.

"What does it matter to you?"

"It doesn't. I am a farmer myself and just thought I could

help on the land. I have extensive experience in agriculture."

"Don't patronise me on my own land!"

"Well you won't let us leave and now I can't make conversation so what do you want me to do?"

The man relaxed for a moment. He folded his arms and stared at Little John who hid behind his leg. "My name is John and I see you have met my son."

"Must I say what a fine young boy you have."

"Not really. He has a heart more tender than a woman's. He needs to toughen up. If he was a man, he would have cast you both away. Let alone tell me we had intruders on the land. What do you want from here anyway?"

Henry stepped forward. "My sister isn't well and she needs help. I won't let my town banish her to the York Retreat. I am trying to save her before it's too late and I know time is running out. Will you help me?"

"What's in it for me?"

"My horse."

Henry pointed at Ginny from between the shrubs, who laid in the same position the prior day. Her black mane shone in the evening light as her head was laid to rest. John examined the horse from afar and nodded his head. "She is a working horse and used to farming the land, ploughing and whatever else you need her for. I give you my word."

John raised an eyebrow. "Is your horse worth that little?"

"No but I am desperate."

"I have no idea what you want me to do."

"I have the instructions from a Scarborough doctor for a purge but I cannot do it alone. I need another set of hands."

John looked down at his son who fiddled with the buckle of his suspenders. "I shall give my final verdict tomorrow morning."

Henry gulped, he could only hope John would uphold his end of the bargain.

# Chapter Twelve

----------------------

## False Pretence

John stomped through the barn and stood before Henry. The awful stench of rotten potatoes floated from his mouth. "You sold me a faulty horse!" He bellowed.

"Do not accuse me of such a crime! My horse is of the best quality, don't tarnish my name!"

"That horse," John pointed. "Has a broken leg. It's good for nothing."

Henry held his breath and stared at John's missing-a-tooth grin. John thrust him to the floor and kicked him over. "Get out of here!"

Henry lay still for a moment, he needed to think and quick. Time was short and John's patience had almost disappeared. Henry leapt to his feet and extended his hand backwards, shielding Emery from the fight. "Let me make you a new proposition and one you cannot deny. I see you are missing a tooth. I will sell you my own as well as the broken gelding."

John burrowed a frown. He appeared both offended and pleased by the proposition. He thought for a short while. "Alright. I want your front tooth and then we can help your sister. I know a dentist," he grinned.

Emery grabbed Henry's forearm. "I won't let you do this. I am not worth it."

"Of course you are."

"No, if I wasn't your sister then you wouldn't do this for me."

"Well obviously. This man is our last hope, I can't do the purge alone."

"Sell him my tooth."

"Nonsense," Henry scoffed.

"I am serious."

Henry spun around. "This journey was my idea, everything that happens must go through me. I won't let anyone hurt you."

Henry tried to smile but his lips were frozen shut. He was almost as mad as Emery. He lost more than he thought possible on the journey to save her. But he couldn't look back now. Losing a tooth was a small sacrifice to make. Even so, he was a coward. Petrified of the pain but too prideful to admit it. He couldn't walk away from the trade off of his tooth.

The dentist entered the barn, with nothing other than a single metal tool in hand. He gestured to the chair and Henry sat down. He dug his nails into the handles of the chair and listened to his own breaths. The dentist examined the polished forceps; a silver metal clamp. He wiped away a mark by a linen cloth and nodded. His chunky hand pressed Henry's forehead backwards and the dentist tapped his tooth. Henry's mouth grew dry and he was desperate for a drink of water. He swallowed nothing but air as the dentist examined him. It appeared too small for John's oversized mouth but it would still make a fine denture.

John folded his arms and grinned at the prize which would soon be his. Once this was over, the purge could be performed and only then would Emery be saved. The journey was almost complete. This was it.

The dentist secured a firm hold against Henry's forehead, pressing his head back. He clasped the forceps around the tooth and pulled. A blunt ache radiated from Henry's mouth and he groaned. His nails dug into the chair until it splintered whilst the tooth was twisted counter clockwise and blood soon filled his mouth. He gagged against the metallic taste.

The dentist paused but not from pity. He re-angled the clamp and then pulled downright against the tooth. Oblivious to Henry's cry.

From the corner of the barn, John pulled up a chair beside Emery and Little John. They all awaited the extraction to come to an end. Their patience annoyed Henry, they just watched while he suffered. Although, he knew why he was doing it and focused on that.

He gasped for air and shut his eyes. Pain radiated from his face. He clawed at the chair handles. His calloused fingers pressed against the wood, when a sharp pain pricked his finger. A splinter was lodged inside. He drew his finger back and balled a fist. He tried to focus on something else but his mind was consumed with so much pain, that it was virtually impossible.

The dentist tugged down on the tooth. Henry mumbled as an elbow was shoved into his shoulder. He was pushed lower into the chair.

"Hold still," the dentist complained.

Henry pushed his back into the seat. Trying to hold still. Although the pain was almost numbing, he grew accustomed to it.

Minutes later the tooth was extracted. Henry dropped forward and clutched his mouth, it was done. Blood and saliva dripped from Henry's mouth.

"The purge," he spat.

The barn was filled with make-shift crosses. Without a priest, they had no choice but to make the barn resemble a holy place. Henry twisted a thread of rope around two twigs, tying them together to form another cross. He realised Little John stared at him, whilst he toyed with the buckle of his suspenders. Henry cocked his head and the boy ran over.

Henry crouched down, with two sticks in hand. "I'll teach you how to make a cross. First of all, hold them together like this."

Little John held one stick upright and the other horizontal. "Like this?" He asked.

"Good job. Hold them still while I loop this thread around them."

Henry worked to secure the twigs in place but Little John's arms obviously got tired and his grip loosened. The cross was at an angle. It would have to do.

"Can we hang it over there?" Little John exclaimed.

Henry chuckled and hoisted Little John atop his shoulders. They walked over to the doorway, where there was a wooden beam above the entrance. "Can you reach?" Henry asked.

Little John leaned forward and placed the wonky cross on the beam.

"Henry!" John called. He threw him a tallow candle. Herny knew what had to be done.

Candles chased away the darkness but consumed the warehouse with the smell of lard and essential lavender oil. Emery's hands were strapped to a wooden chair. She faced the floor as her feet were immersed into the hay ground. Henry crouched down and tried to look into her eyes but she turned away. He laid his hand over hers. The fear was almost palpable. Even so, she nodded, she knew this was for the better.

"I'm right here with you. Everything will be okay once we cast out the demons."

Henry hung a string rope around her neck. The wooden cross now dangled before her chest. He held a set of the rosary beads and walked away. Near the rear end, John skimmed over the purge instructions and wore a white coat. A brass metal cross hung from his neck and he glanced up at Henry. The men exchanged a nod.

"I have never done this before," John whispered. The tooth suited him, a little small but he now bore a friendlier smile.

"I have only seen this done once. I think I know what to do." Henry said. "Somewhat."

He grabbed the glass bottle filled with holy water and walked over to Little John. He crouched down and said, "listen to me boy, whatever you see, whatever you hear, don't be afraid."

Little John tilted his head to the side, he seemed to understand enough of what was to come. His petite pink lips drew apart and he inhaled a deep breath. Then he nodded and decided to hold back the questions.

Henry unscrewed the lid from the holy water and looked upright.

*Tonight we will illuminate the path through the darkness. I summon angels into this place, I welcome their divinity.*

John tightened his grasp around the letter. "O glorious archangels defend our battle against the impurities and evil within this place." He paused, and looked over at Henry, with his head held high but the brown eyes glimmered with fear.

Henry thrust splashes of holy water onto Emery. She flinched as the cold water fell onto her skin. He circled her, repeatedly dousing her in water. Black hair covered his face and his emerald eyes glistened from the candlelight. His boots crunched over the straw and the sound made Emery shudder.

"I don't like this," Little John's squeaky voice said. He watched the purge unfold. He tugged at Henry's shirt but was ignored. Henry had to focus on summoning the trinity into the barn. He listened to John's prayer and felt every word. The purge was far more important than Little John's endless string of questions that he would soon ask.

Emery's eyes darted around the room; it seemed she was searching for a distraction for him. Then she leant forward and licked her eyes on him. "We are playing a game. Do you like games?"

Little John nodded.

"Can you count how many crosses are in this room?"

He walked along the circumference of the barn and pointed to the crosses made of twigs and sticks. Emery watched him calmly. Her eyes followed him and she was pleased to focus on something other than the purge. Then she thrust her head to the side. Her lips moved. She listened to the voices, they were near. Her puffed cheeks and John chanted louder than before. She panted, trying to fight off the whispers. Emery looked the other way. She struggled against the straps around her wrists and ankles. She groaned inside her mouth.

"I found Six!" Little John exclaimed with his hands clasped behind his back.

A tear ran down Emery's cheek. She was suddenly still. "Seven. You forgot the most important one." She nodded at the wonky cross above the doorway. "That's my favourite cross."

John continued, "fight this day, through the battle, with the holy angels, Lucifer and the host are powerless against thee. The ancient serpent will be cast into the abyss along with his angels."

Emery snapped her neck the other way and whispered but her voice trembled and was too faint to understand. She bowed her head and spoke to the floor. The conversation seemed to switch between languages and the words spat from her lips. Saliva dribbled to the floor and her teeth chattered.

Henry splashed the holy water over her body. He swallowed his fear and focused on Emery. It had to be done. He fought the urge to crouch down and reassure her everything would be alright.

John bellowed louder and the prayer echoed off the walls, where Little John cowered beside.

Emery was overwhelmed and wept alone in the room. She stopped whispering and focused on the ground. Besides her pitiful tears, she remained silent and reactionless to the prayer. Emery's broken eyes looked at him, she was tired and humiliated. She shook her head, the purge did not work. Henry didn't know what to expect but it wasn't this. He would know if the purge had worked, he would feel it in his bones. This was not it.

He raised a hand to John, who understood the silent gesture. It was over. He left the barn.

The damp grass felt slimy between Henry's fingers and the cold seeped through his stockings as he sat atop the ground. He sighed before the stars, the same ones that followed him thus far with Emery. They saw him fail and he bowed his head.

After the purge, the farmland was silent, even Ginny was asleep. The slosh of damp shrubs sounded beneath John's boots, who sat beside Henry.

"I'm sorry."

"Don't be," Henry replied.

"I know you never wanted her to go into the York Retreat."

"She isn't going there. If we cannot save her, then she must learn to live with the disease. Everyday, she has to fight it. That may be for the rest of her life but there is no alternative."

"How will she fight it if she has struggled this far?"

"Faith. When I cover her ears and pray, the voices settle. It may not work forever but still proves there is a way out."

John extended his legs and the muddy boots flopped against the ground. He removed the cross around his neck and it lay on the grass like a hopeless reminder of their failure. "She is lucky to have you. I don't know anyone else that would have come this far. You could let her follow the delusions, where she could live in an alternate reality. I don't see any harm in such, so long as she is happy."

Henry cleared his throat and nodded. There was nothing more to be said. The journey had come to an end but the future was more untold than ever. Emery would return home as she was before, unchanged and sick. Henry was wrong to think he could have cured her but he found a way through the darkness. The guardian angels and the trinity would guide a light out of the dim future. That would be Emery's hope.

"I will leave by dawn," Henry said.

"Before you go, would you like your tooth back?"

The men chuckled. Their laughter lifted through the night and echoed down the hill.

"Tell you what," John began. "I like your thinking Henry and, much unlike myself, you are a prosperous farmer."

Henry froze still. The tales he told John were no lie, the produce had almost doubled that year. But nonetheless, he was still a man of poverty. Even John's barn was nicer than Henry's house. The raw emotional pain set in but he concealed it with a smirk.

"I think Little John would enjoy learning from you. That is, if you would allow him to lend a hand on your farm?"

"Only if you agree to a glass of gin every once in a while," Henry smirked. He extended his hand, to which John accepted the handshake.

Henry unscrewed the cap from the bottle of holy water and raised it to his lips. His mouth filled with the essence of water. He passed it to John who stared at him confused.

"There is shame in letting it go to waste."

John chuckled and gulped down the remainder of the holy water. "York is a few hours from here, would you allow me to give you a lift? We can use one of my horses. I will let my wife know where we are headed, Little John will come as well."

# Chapter Thirteen

——————————————-

## Four Fledglings

They were accompanied by two brown horses, led by John's compass. A breeze set in and Henry shuddered. His hands froze still and a tap of his heel navigated the horse in the right direction. There the four of them were; Henry, Emery, John and Little John. Fate crossed their paths and now they journeyed together.

*It's strange, I don't know anything about John but I trust him. He seems to understand. As if he knows the pain of losing someone he loves but I won't ask.*

*I cannot help but think of the four of us as fledglings on a journey; Emery must learn to live with a new meaning, Little John is to learn farming, then John and I seem to guide everyone through the unknown. Although we have no idea what we are doing. We are passengers of what's to come.*

Henry and John navigated the horses through the greenery, as Little John and Emery sat behind each of their backs. The horses were well trained and seemingly young. Almost like Ginny. She had journeyed thus far and now left behind. She would be no use on the farm and more costly to maintain.

Emery's shaky breaths broke through his train of thought. Henry turned around, grabbed her hands and placed them over her ears. "Shut out the voices. Allow them to be no more and now, you must pray for forgiveness."

She prayed in broken sentences with her hands clasped against her ears. A tear ran down her cheek as she fought away the whispers. Henry watched as her breathing soon returned back to normal. He thought about the conversation with John. Perhaps letting her live in an alternate reality wasn't so bad afterall. Even if it was only a temporary solution, it could work.

"You have two choices, Emery. Each time you hear the voices, you can either fight them away or talk back to them. If it's a good voice, have a conversation if you must but just know it's not real. If the voice is taunting you, do as you just did and welcome your faith instead."

John interrupted the conversation. "We are almost at York," he pointed ahead.

Little John peered over his shoulder and squinted into the darkness. He eagerly searched for the town.

A chill shot down Henry's spine. They were almost home but he didn't know what that meant. The journey was over and didn't end as he expected, he only hoped that Emery could be redeemed. Given her current state and coping mechanisms, she would not be sent to the York Retreat. He neither failed nor succeeded, either way the journey was worth it. He looked over at John who returned the stare. Neither of them spoke, for the future was still uncertain. Little John leaned forward and waved at Henry, who chuckled.

"Boy, would you like to work on my farm next week? I could use a hand with cleaning the horses."

Little John turned to his Father, with a grin stretched across his face.

Henry jumped down and watched as John tied the reins of the horses together. The journey had come to an end but sparked a newfound friendship.

"This is it," Henry said.

"Not quite. Although I must leave, I shall stop past next week for that glass of gin? Then, you can tell me all about what happens next," John smirked.

Emery dismantled the horse and stood beside Henry. Her eyes beamed with gratitude and a shadow of angst. In the near distance was their house. The windows were dim and the familiar stench of urine re-appeared. He scoured the farm, the crops were now flourishing and the weeds overgrown. So much had changed in a week. He walked towards the porch where the cream paint peeled off of the pillars that supported the shelter. Henry exhaled and watched his cold breath evaporate. The wind chilled his face but not as much as the fear that curdled within his stomach. He turned to Emery, who was stone cold. She picked at her nail beds and the sound of her nails scratching emitted. Her lips drew apart but she seemed to choke on her own words before she finally spoke.

"It's okay, you know, if I must return to the cellar. I got out for a while," she faced the ground.

Henry leant forward.

"Don't try to comfort me. From here, whatever is, will be."

She grabbed the door handle and twisted it open.

# Chapter Fourteen

----------------

## Exiled

Henry crept through the house and the floor creaked. His heart pumped at the back of his throat. It didn't seem like home. They were strangers to the house. He felt along the walls and guided them to the kitchen, where a stream of light crept from between the curtains. The hole in the wall was now covered by a piece of cardboard and the smell of mould surrounded the room. He turned on the tap and cupped his hands. He splashed icy water over his face and washed away the journey but the memory of his failure remained.

The English Setter appeared and sniffed Henry's pants. It's wet nose trailed across his body. He reached a hand down and patted its head. The Setter licked away the water from Henry's hand. "Good dog."

Emery trailed her fingers along the kitchen benchtop. She sniffled as she remembered her life before. All the family dinners, days spent cooking with mother, birthdays and homemade cakes that were cut in the kitchen. She even missed out on her own birthday last year. It was spent alone in the cellar, until her twin brothers brought her a single piece of stale cake. The kitchen brought her so much joy, once before.

"Why did you come back?" A familiar voice said from the shadows.

It was Father. The husky voice was riddled with anger. The rhetorical question hung in the air. Henry stared out the window, at the morning fog. There was a clearing among the weeds and parsnip sprouted from the freshly upturned soil. The single gelding horse munched on the grass in the nearby paddock, it was without company. That damned horse now had to carry the farmland.

A metallic taste lined Henry's mouth and he spat into the sink. Blood stained his saliva. The tooth had not yet healed from the extraction. Great. He would eat mashed food for the next week.

"Did you think I would not return?" Henry finally asked.

"I really wish you didn't," father spat.

"Why? So you could get rid of your problems? You could have finally made Emery disappear, just like you always wanted. You probably wanted to make me go away too. Rid the family of the shame I've brought."

"If you won't set things right, then I will."

"Let go of me!" Emery wailed. Henry spun around to see Father grab her forearm and head down the hallway. She screamed and dropped to the floor.

Henry closed in on them and thrust Father's hands away. The men stared each other down. Father's eyes were glum and dark. He raised a finger to Henry and snarled to reveal rows of grey teeth.

"How dare you. Who do you think you are, Henry? One thing is for sure, you're not my son."

"I helped her more than you ever would!"

The Setter barked from nearby. It bore a set of pointed canine teeth and jumped around the kitchen.

"What did you do?" Father grabbed Henry's shirt and dragged him closer. "She looks worse than ever! Malnourished and dazed. Not to mention you lost my gelding! The bloody horse isn't in my front paddock. You know we can't afford another, so where is it?"

"The horse was traded to save Emery. Surely you would do the same for your daughter."

Father twisted Henry's collar. The cuff choked him but he kept a straight face. Then he was flung sidewards and his head smacked into the wall. The blunt force radiated pain from the backside of his head. Emery cupped her hands over her mouth and muffled a scream. She darted to the farside of the kitchen and cowered behind the table.

"Let go of me," Henry gasped. "I tried to save her, just like the doctor suggested."

"Then you are just as much of a fool. You turned against the orders of the priest. But I won't. I lead this family. I make the decisions, not you!"

Father clenched his fist and plunged forward. Smack. Henry's nose cracked and thick blood oozed down his face. He wailed and clenched his jaw.

"I disown both of you." Father punched Henry in the face and again. His vision blurred until Father's face was muddled and only recognizable by the grunts powered by his punches. "I'll send you to the York Retreat too. You are just as mad."

Henry's head pounded and his blood vessels throbbed with agony. He gasped for air as Father strangled his throat. His lips gulped like a fish.

"I had to make up a story for the entire town! Everyone has been asking where you are and why Emery is suddenly so silent. What did you expect me to tell them?"

Henry's hands felt along the bench. He was hardly conscious and his head spun into a blur. He was desperate for a way out. His sweaty fingertips encircled something, although he wasn't sure what it was. He wheezed for air and stared at the ceiling. His fingers quivered and quickly lost strength. Once he reconfigured himself, he grabbed a knife and thrust it into the air. Henry felt the knife slam into something and Father gurgled.

He gasped for air and his chest expanded uncomfortably. He refocused on the roof. The detailed ceiling soon appeared clear again. He then realised Father was no longer standing before him. Emery emerged from behind the table. She tripped over her own feet and shrieked at the top of her lungs.

Henry stared at her confused and then he followed her gaze. Lying on the ground was his Father's limp body. His face was haloed by crimson blood. He did not breathe or move. Henry dropped to his knees, to see there was a hole in Father's neck. His hands shook. To his dismay, a knife dropped from his hand. It fell to the floor.

Emery dragged herself across the floor and shook Father's body. An endless string of words drooled from her lips. She planted her face into the lifeless chest and cried.

The Setter yelped and ran towards the body. His ears pressed back and his tail stood still. He searched over Father and vigorously licked the body. Crimson blood spurted over his face and dyed his fur red. The Setter pressed his snout into the wound from Father's neck and helplessly licked away the blood.

*I didn't mean it. By my own hands I am a murderer but it's not my fault. I see the angst in Emery's eyes as she watches me. Like I am a monster, which I am not. I wish I could make her forget. If only I could undo everything. Angels, show me the light. Guide me out of this endless string of sin. Take away this pain.*

Henry stumbled backwards and collided into the wall. The fresh blood licked his boots as he now stood in a puddle of his own mess. His heart compressed within his own chest and his bones quivered with ache. Father was dead. Footsteps immediately ran down the hallway.

"What have you done?" Urian bellowed. He stood in the doorway barefoot and dressed in a pair of striped pajamas. His face was stone pale and his jaw dropped open. His marched forward and slapped Henry across the face. The burn was obsolete compared to the yearning pain from within. Although, the slap seemed to have submerged a flood of guilt. He could almost hear his own heartbeat.

"What the hell have you done? Returned after some weeks and now you killed our Father!" Urian roared.

"I didn't mean to harm him. I - I," Henry stumbled. There wasn't an answer for what had unfolded. No explanation for the truth.

"You bloody idiot! How could you?" Urian wailed. His eyes were black and unforgiving. "You shamed this family and now you are no longer one of us."

The patter of bare feet ran down the house. Dread filled Henry. Everything was about to get much worse.

"Mother, don't come in here!" Henry wailed.

"Why not?" Her voice echoed down the corridor.

Urian blocked her with an extended arm. He stood in the doorway. He wrapped his arms around Mother, to stop her from moving. She peeked over his shoulder and her knees caved in. She broke out of the tight grasp.

The sound of her petite voice made Henry want to disappear forever. Shaken breaths parted from his chapped lips as he froze still. There was nowhere to run. Nowhere to hide. He had to face the repercussions of his doing.

Mother bellowed the most animalistic cry of all. She dropped to her knees and scurried across the floor. Her hands were soon drenched in blood and she wept into Father's face. Tears dripped into his mouth and her wails echoed.

"Get out of here!" She bellowed. Her voice was hoarse and the screams burned her throat. "All of you, get out of here!"

Bile scorched the back of Henry's throat. He darted towards the bathroom and emptied his stomach contents into the chamber pot. He clutched his head, it spununcontrollably. It all happened too fast for him to grab a hold of the situation. None of it felt real but the crippling pain said otherwise. A tear fell from his chin, he ruined everything, whilst trying to mend the family. From the doorway, footsteps ran down the house. He gulped down the remainder of vomit and followed them into the bedroom. Henry stumbled across the house and used the walls for stability.

Behind the opaque curtains Urian's shadow manoeuvred. He opened a drawer and then slammed it shut. Henry pressed his head against the wall and his lips moved but he did not speak. He panted through the nausea, somehow, hoping it wasn't true.

"I never want to speak to you again," Urian said. "I am leaving, I can't stay here anymore. You have destroyed our lives more than I thought possible."

"Please, it was an accident."

"I don't care. I am leaving, I will have to make a life for myself. It's not like I can marry in this town now or sell our produce. Nobody would buy from a murderous family. Don't you dare follow me, or I will kill you myself."

"Where would you go? Winchester? Scarborough?" Henry scoured Urian's face, waiting for a reaction that never came. He paused. "Norwich?"

Urian looked away.

"You're going all the way to Norwich, aren't you?"

"Yes." Urian rounded the curtain with a suitcase by his feet. He grabbed Henry's face and pulled him close. The twins were ripped apart and would probably never be the same again. They listened to the screams from the kitchen, which grew louder and a burning tear fell from Henry's eye.

"I know you didn't do this on purpose, I can feel it. But I can't forgive you," Urian whispered.

"Don't disappear, Urian. I need you."

"Did you save Emery?"

"Somewhat. Please let me come with you. I can't stay here. I can't stand the way our mother looked at me. She was filled with hatred and despise."

Urian pointed at Henry. "Don't you even think of walking away. You must stay here and set things right. Our widowed mother needs someone to run this farm and bring home an income. If you dare leave her and Emery alone, I will be out of your life for good. This is the very least that you can do."

"She doesn't want me here! I would only cause more pain if I stayed!"

"Pain is temporary! She is a mess, you need to take care of her. Emery is useless. She is sicker than ever before. So, that leaves you, brother. Take care of them."

Urian bowed his head and an oxygen-depriving heaviness filled the room. Henry yearned to leave, to flee his sin and hide away.

"What would you do if you were me?"

Urian ignored the question. "I'll write to you, brother. I just can't look at you right now," Urian mumbled. He pushed past Henry and his luggage trailed along the floor.

Henry dropped to the floor. He wanted nothing more than to disappear.

# Chapter Fifteen

----------------------

## The Prairie

*The gin changes nothing but for a brief moment I forget who I am and what I have done. My head spins and an involuntary grin stretches across my face. I am nothing but a puppet, pretending all is normal on the farm. But I know the truth. Father is buried in the soil beneath my feet. Below the wooden patio, he rests in peace.*

The sun glistened over the porch and Henry shielded his eyes. In the distance a meek figure moved repetitively, upturning the soil, ploughing into the night. He turned to John who extended a lit cigarette and Henry accepted. Trails of smoke danced together, forming one body.

"How has your mother been doing since Mister Gilchrist left?" John asked.

"She will be okay again ... Someday. She hasn't said much and stays locked inside the bedroom but she has made an appearance. I think she is improving."

"I still can't believe your father took off. He didn't say where he was going?"

"No," Henry gulped, "just that he would be gone for a while."

He slipped his bandaged hand into his coat, not wanting to start another topic for conversation. The injuries he sustained from the fight would soon heal and Father's disappearance would no longer be unusual. The town would grow used to the idea that he left for business.

John examined his empty glass of gin. "Allow me to fetch us some more."

"Do you know where it is?"

John nodded and disappeared inside the house. Henry pulled a pen and piece of paper out of his coat. He began to write, it seemed like a good time. It had been a few weeks since Urian left and it was about time he responded to the previous letter. His fingers slipped over the pen, the words would not come easy this time. Perhaps this was the twins' newfound relationship although it was anything but normal. Henry scoured the letter, searching for answers on the page.

Little John whipped the sweat from his forehead and dropped the plough. In time, he would build strength and learn to plough properly. He walked towards the patio with his baggy overalls that had a broken link. He plonked into the seat beside Henry and kicked off his boots. He looked over, trying to smile behind the fatigue.

"Who is Emery talking to, is she crazy?" Little John asked.

Henry switched his gaze to the farm, in the distance was Emery. She walked across the open plains, toes in the sand. Her silk white gown tumbled in the wind and black hair was pressed over shoulders and contorted in the breeze. The wind whistled and Henry listened as she whispered to the twilight:

"Across this prairie we walk until the end of time. As if we are a peaceful painting, frozen in place. I hear you, Father. I hear you once more. Tread this place once more. For all of time …"

The words blew into the distance. Henry transcribed the sight onto the pages. He knew what to write. The words flowed and it now seemed obvious.

Little John breathed against Henry's neck whilst he stared at the letter. "What does it say?"

Henry took the letter in both hands and cleared his throat. He read:

*I suppose the best way to write to you, brother, is by what I see and so, what I see is right now our farmland. It is flourishing again and should bring in a decent paycheck. I have acquired a new friend who is helping and in exchange, I teach him what I know. Everything that we learnt together. He is not you and will never be a replacement but I could use the extra help. Mother is learning to live again, she even smiled for the first time the other day. Although, she resents me, as she should. I can't say life has been fortunate since you left. Mother fights against my presence every single day. She hates me but is slowly realising my value on the farm. She needs me to cultivate the land. I hope than one day she remembers me as her son and not a murderer. I hope that day is not too far away. But none of us have forgotten our Father, who is at rest for all of eternity. As for our dear sister, Emery, she has found a new peace. Not as we might have expected but she is cured in another way. She converses with the voices, every day. She hears our deceased Father's voice in the wind. She walks barefoot across the endless prairie and talks back to him. I see no harm in feeding this delusion. The cure all along, was to let Emery live in her own hallucinations, so long as they are joyous. Since the accident, she has not complained as much of the demonic voices. I suppose faith plays a role in this but so does her newfound coping mechanism. She closes her eyes and covers her ears. Emery has learnt they are fake. Of course, some days are worse than others. But she lives life with new meaning. I am here to facilitate her journey. I will always be there for support and to remind her, the voices are not real. On better days, she speaks to Father. He is with her, he is with all of us, even if we do not see it. She alters between two realities but to her it is all the same. So, what I see is that Emery is happy and so, she is home, forevermore.*

*Until we speak again,*

*Henry Gilchrist.*

www.ingramcontent.com/pod-product-compliance
Lightning Source LLC
Chambersburg PA
CBHW060427260626
47161CB00005B/1820